SHERLOCK HOLMES MYS

VOLUME 1, NUMBER 3

I'm sorry, sir, but the embezzler position
has already been filled.

Publisher: *John Betancourt*
Editor: *Marvin Kaye*
Managing Editor: Stephen H. Segal

Sherlock Holmes Mystery Magazine is published by Wildside
Press, LLC. Single copies: $10.00 + postage. Subscriptions: $29.95 for
the next 3 issues in the U.S.A., from:
Wildside Press LLC, Subscription Dept.
9710 Traville Gateway Dr., #234; Rockville MD 20850

An electronic edition is available from Fictionwise.
www.fictionwise.com.

FROM WATSON'S SCRAPBOOK

After Holmes perused the second issue of *Sherlock Holmes Mystery Magazine,* I felt considerable relief to discover that he did not altogether dislike it. Here I must confess my rôle in these proceedings; it was I who persuaded Holmes to lend his name to this periodical. Of course I offered him an equal portion in the honorarium agreed upon with the publisher, but Holmes generously declined, only stipulating that I keep a keen eye upon the contents.

This is an issue I have discussed carefully with Mr Kaye, who, as editor, selects what appears in each number. Leading the mix each time, of course, is one of my own accounts of Holmes's many adventures, followed by recountings by other authors of some of our exploits that I did not get around to recording myself. In these cases, I have provided these scribes with my own notes, together with whatever verbal addenda they may require.

So far, so good. But in the preceding issue, Mr Kaye also elected to include a tale not only associated with that fellow Stoker's infamous vampire, but was actually narrated by a *cat.* I tried to talk Mr Kaye out of publishing it, but I am glad, and as stated above, relieved to learn that not only did not Holmes object to "The Adventure of the Hanoverian Vampires," he found it mildly risible.

"Watson, Watson," he chided me, "the author obviously wrote it with tongue in cheek. An amusing bit of fluff it is, hardly likely to damage the reputation I owe in good part to you, my dear fellow."

Holmes's charity notwithstanding, I am pleased to note that the current issue of *Sherlock Holmes Mystery Magazine* restricts itself to more traditional Holmesian fare, beginning with my own work, "The Adventure of the Speckled Band," and proceeding to that rare instance of Holmes himself narrating a story, the now-it-can-be-told adventure, "Watson's Wound," ably edited by Bruce Kilstein from Holmes's difficult-to-decipher handwriting. (Perhaps I shouldn't comment, given the abysmal reputation of physician penmanship.)

I should explain why Mr Kaye chose to use the "Speckled Band" case in this, the third issue. He has elected to follow the dating of my stories as postulated by William S. Baring-Gould in his classic tome (or tomes, depending upon which edition one owns), *The Annotated Sherlock Holmes.* Thus, earlier issues have featured Holmes's first two cases, the "Gloria Scott" and "The Musgrave Ritual." According to Baring-Gould, the next in line ought to be *A Study in Scarlet,* in which is recounted how Holmes and I first met, as well how Holmes solved the murder of one Enoch J Drebber of America.

Mr Kaye and I discussed this and came to the conclusion that as *A Study in Scarlet* is a novel, its length, even broken into two installments, would crowd out other compositions waiting to appear in these pages. Inasmuch as it is readily available elsewhere, it was decided to skip over it and go on to the next of our adventures, that of the "Speckled Band."

However, in lieu of my first Holmes novel, we have, instead, Kim Newman's "A Volume in Vermillion." Mr Newman, a fellow Brit, somehow managed to get his hands on a till-now unpublished manuscript by no less a villain than Colonel Sebastian Moran, whom you may recall was referred to by Holmes as "the second most dangerous man in London." Thanks to Mr Newman's efforts, a nefarious plan of his formidable employer comes to light for the first time, one that had its impact on *A Study in* Scarlet, to the utter astonishment of both Holmes and myself!

I began with a confession, and must end with the same. I am glad our erstwhile landlady Mrs Hudson has elected to alter the nature of her ongoing column in these pages. Holmes and I were a tad dismayed at the advice feature she wrote for the past two issues, thus we are pleased to see that she has elected to alter the nature of her column. "Frankly," she told me, "it was becoming rather a bore. In future, I shall restrict myself to suggestions of a more practical nature . . . useful hints for tending a well-ordered household." At my urging, she has consented to include more of those splendid recipes that Holmes and I enjoyed at our Baker Street digs.

And now I yield the floor to Mr Kaye.

— John H Watson, M D

It's a pleasure to welcome back our columnist Lenny Picker, as well as Gary Lovisi, who gave us an excellent Holmesian tale last issue; this time Gary shares his passion for collecting scarce and rare Holmes books.

Bob Byrne contributes an article introducing Mr Nero Wolfe, as if he needs any such thing . . . and yet I am always dismayed to learn how many avid mystery buffs have not read Rex Stout's novels and stories about the only American detective worthy to be named as an equal to Sherlock Holmes. When this magazine was first contemplated by its publisher John Betancourt and myself, we seriously considered titling it the *Nero Wolfe Mystery Magazine,* but it was ultimately determined that Holmes's name would (hopefully) attract more readers. In future, though, I do hope to include more articles about Wolfe, as well as stories.

I have received several e-mails requesting guidelines for submission. I have not prepared any, nor shall I; I do not like to put restraints upon writers, and as a result I am often happily surprised. In the first issue, I outlined what we are striving to make the magazine; said information, slightly expanded, appears below. However, I am not reading new submissions at this time; our inventory is fully stocked at present.

When I accepted the editorship of *Sherlock Holmes Mystery Magazine*, I had two models in mind: *Ellery Queen's Mystery Magazine*, especially in its earlier years, when it and *The Magazine of Fantasy and Science Fiction* provided me with a liberal, detailed fund of knowledge about their respective genres. My second model was the old *London Mystery Magazine*, which ran from 1949 to 1982.

I began reading *EQMM* during my graduate days at Penn State. My late friend Professor Ellis Grove gifted me with a huge number of issues dating back to at least the 1940s. (Alas, I lost them in a Wilkes-Barre PA flood!) Despite its name, it was, of course, a magazine containing a wide range of detective and crime stories, and that ultimately is what *SHMM* is all about.

So, to quote my first editorial, "while Watsonian pastiches and spoofs will appear as often as the merit of such submissions deserve, they will be counterbalanced by new mystery stories, period pieces, tales of murder and other crimes, puzzle/riddle tales if anyone still writes them, and in short, mysteries set in the present, past, and possibly even the future." I lament the dearth of classic "reader solvable" mystery stories complete with clues and red herrings; any of those submitted will be highly regarded, and I have been fortunate to have received a few, though more often submissions are crime stories *sans* the kind of clue-stashing so ably executed by Bill DeAndrea, Anthony Boucher, Agatha Christie, Carter Dickson, etc., etc.

The reason *London Mystery Magazine* is cited as a model is because that venerable publication interpreted "mystery" to include an occasional foray into the supernatural. Now this is something that sometimes irritates avid mystery buffs (John Dickson Carr comes to mind as an author who was not afraid to mix the two), so out of respect to this putative readership, such fiction will only appear occasionally in *Sherlock Holmes Mystery Magazine*.

With the above in mind, in this issue you will find, in addition to the stories Watson cited above, a period piece by Darrell Schweitzer, "The Death of Falstaff"; a hard-boiled adventure, Stan Trybulski's "Tough Guys Don't Pay"; a miniature classic detective tale, "Vacation from Crime," which brings back Hal Charles's delightful TV news anchor Kelly Locke and her Chief-of-Detectives father — the pair appeared in our first issue, and will be back again in the future. Also in this issue is "Workout" by the late Jean Paiva, a fantasy with a murderer unlike any you've ever encountered.

Our final story, "Mayhem in St Margaret Mede," is a splendid spoof of TV's classic espionage adventure, *The Avengers*. I contracted for it to run in our second issue, but a computer crash destroyed the file; all that remained was the title and its author, whose e-address no longer was valid. After endless phone calls, I managed to track Peter King down, thanks to a newspaper editor in Sarasota; Peter resubmitted the file; and here it is, at long last!

N. B. for readers who also may be copy editors — In the same fashion that this publication eschews "Sherlockian" in favour of "Holmesian," which is the preferred term in England, so do we respect Dr. Watson's Britishisms (which also appear in my editorials, and any article or story whose author prefers words with "u" such as "favour" or "honour"). In keeping with Watsonian as well as Dickensian style, there is an absence of periods in such usages as Mr, Mrs, Dr, and after middle initials, such as the above-mentioned Enoch J Drebber

Canonically yours,
Marvin Kaye

Please do not send manuscripts to the publisher or they will be returned unread. At the present time, our inventory is full. When the editor asks for additional submissions, they should go to him at his e-mail address.

THE NON-SOLITARY CYCLISTS

The Screen of the Crime

by Lenny Picker

Not many experts on Sherlock Holmes would rank "The Adventure of the Solitary Cyclist" as one of the best stories in the Canon. Arthur Conan Doyle himself omitted it from his own ranking of the top nineteen short Holmes stories; and in his prologue to his account of the case, good old Watson frankly noted that, "It is true that the circumstance did not admit of any striking illustration of those powers for which my friend was famous," before adding that "there were some points about the case which made it stand out." My recent re-reading of the tale supports the Doctors's two opinions. While the central puzzle — why does an unknown bearded man follow Violet Smith as she cycles between Charlington Hall and Farnham Station? — is an intriguing one, the resolution is much less so. After some atypical violence — the Master's pub fight with the odious, over-the-top villain, Mr. Woodley, and some gunplay, Holmes foils the criminal's schemes by being in the right place at the right time — and he is almost too late. And his deductions about the reason for Miss Smith's shadow are less impressive than in "The Adventure of the Copper Beeches," another damsel-in-distress short story.

Despite these deficiencies, "The Solitary Cyclist" was one of the major inspirations for what I contend is one of the best Sherlock Holmes films of all time — although neither Holmes nor Watson appear in it. But the "curious incident of the Holmes" in the *Murder Rooms* is easily explainable. The 2001 BBC adaptation of David

Pirie's superior novel, *The Patient's Eyes: The Dark Beginnings of Sherlock Holmes,* is one of a series constructed from Piries's premise that the real-life model for the Master, Edinburgh's Dr. Joseph Bell, did actual detection, aided by a young Arthur Conan Doyle. Considering it a Holmes film is, for me, an easy call, especially after enduring, albeit with an occasional chortle, viewing the execrable 1962 German-French-Italian production, *Sherlock Holmes and the Deadly Necklace*, with its badly-dubbed dialogue and a jazzy musical score that has to be heard to be believed, in an ill-fated effort to craft a column examining screen adaptations of *The Valley of Fear*, for which the world is not yet prepared. Just because Christopher Lee plays a character called Holmes in the movie (with the addition of a very obvious prosthetic nose, and with someone else voicing his lines in English), doesn't make it worthy of serious discussion as a Sherlock Holmes film, unless the subject is Screen Adaptations Of The Works Of Arthur Conan Doyle — Unintended Humor In. By contrast, in my opinion, the episode of *Murder Rooms: The Dark Beginnings of Sherlock Holmes* entitled "The Patient's Eyes" has it all: intelligent writing, brilliant acting, especially from the three leads; outstanding production values; and a carefully-constructed plot. For those readers who have not yet seen it, I hope this column will convince you to buy, or at least rent it on DVD, as well as seek out the novel.

A fictional Bell/Doyle pairing had been attempted before in Howard Engel's 1997s novel *Mr. Doyle and Dr. Bell*, an inferior book in which the doctor and his protegé race the clock to save a man from the gallows. But there's no comparison between Engel's work and Pirie's. The latter, a British screenwriter, film producer, film critic, and novelist, whose previous work included a 1997s adaptation of Wilkie Collins's *The Woman In White*, made a careful study of Doyle's early life in constructing his historical fictions.

Pirie had asked himself, "What is it with Holmes that he has such an uncanny reality about him? Reading the stories undoubtedly brings us closer to the truth, for they have an odd and unexpected intensity. There is a genuine emotion in Doyle's portrayal of Holmes and Watson, which explains some of its impact, but makes the creative origins of this emotion even more mysterious." He began to wonder whether "Holmes seems real because, in certain respects we are only just starting to appreciate, he was real?"

For Pirie, Sherlock Holmes was a product of Doyle's difficult early life. He was well aware of Doyle's letter to the charismatic teacher and physician Joseph Bell, who taught him at Edinburgh University, which stated, "It is certainly to you that I owe Sherlock Holmes." But for Pirie, there was a psychological background to the Bell-Doyle connection. As he has written: "And so it was that Doyle started his early years at Edinburgh medical school with a father who was deranged and whose condition had to be kept secret and now, in the same house, an arrogant older rival for his mother's affection, a man who had succeeded at the profession he was only just beginning. He seems at first to have been deeply alienated from the university. But at this critical time, when Doyle, by his own admission, was feeling wild, full-blooded, and a trifle reckless, someone else appeared: a teacher opposite in every way to these other troublesome fathers. And his name was Joseph Bell."

From this foundation, Pirie crafted a fictionalized Bell and Doyle, spinning engaging narratives taking off from the evidence that the real Bell did assist the official authorities in solving crimes, much as Holmes did. He further imagined that "Bell may have supplied Doyle with some of the actual details of criminal investigation he later put to such good use," in stories like "The Solitary Cyclist."

The first fruit of Pirie's efforts was the 2000 BBC telefilm, *Murder Rooms*, which showed how Bell and Doyle met at the University of Edinburgh, and teamed up to track down a serial killer whose methods anticipated those of Jack the Ripper. Ian Richardson, who had played Holmes in middling 1980s television film adaptations of *The Hound of the Baskervilles* and *The Sign of the Four*, was perfectly cast as Bell, managing to imbue the character with humor and passion to accompany his formidable intellect. Robin Laing, a relative unknown, played Doyle. (While *Murder Rooms* is available on DVD, some significant footage, aired when it was first shown on PBS, has been cut.)

The novel of "The Patient's Eyes" alluded to those events; and it expanded on the telefilm's account of the beginning of the Bell-Doyle team. It cleverly uses elements from "The Solitary Cyclist," "The Speckled Band," and "Wisteria Lodge," as Doyle, some years removed from the trauma that marked the ending of his first investigation as Bell's assistant, attempts to start a new life on the South Coast. He soon finds himself at odds with his employer, Dr. Cullingworth, who values profits over his patients' health. (This character's name, derived from Doyle's "The Stark-Munro Letters," was changed to Turnavine in the screenplay, one of the real names of the man who exploited Doyle in his early days as a doctor.) Despite himself, Doyle falls for one of his patients, Heather Grace, who consults him about an eye problem, and then confides that she has been shadowed by a cloaked figure on a bike. Doyle lies in wait for her pursuer, almost exactly as Watson did in "The Solitary Cyclist," but when, on his second attempt, he spots the person, the man inexplicably vanishes from view. Bell, who has learned of Grace's problem via a letter from Doyle, arrives on the scene and takes command of the case. As the situation escalates to murder, the roster of suspects expands to include not only Cullingworth, Grace's former physician, whose advances were repulsed by her, but Grace's uncle and guardian, Charles Blythe, and her would-be fiancée, Guy Greenwell. The plot is so carefully constructed that it would do a great disservice to those who have neither read the novel nor seen the film to say much more about it. (Those who have who are interested in engaging me on the ending are welcome to email me — my address is at the end of the column.)

Pirie's adaptation of his own work is excellent; it manages to capture the creepy essence of the book in a fast-paced 90 minutes that never lags. The translation of prose into visuals helps accentuate the subtle variations the writer has wrought upon Doyle's original. For example, where Violet Smith's scary journey is on a path bordered by woods on one side and an open field on the other, Pirie has substituted more woods for the field, creating, from the outset, a more oppressive atmosphere that parallels the tormented inner life of Heather Grace, whose parents were brutally murdered years earlier.

And in the opening scene, Grace's cycling is initially unaccompanied by background music, creating a feeling of isolation and loneliness just from the sounds of nature, added to by a momentary glimpse of an abandoned gibbet on the side of her path. Her pursuer appears suddenly close on her heels, before the series's haunting theme music is introduced. And rather than merely a man "clad in a dark suit," with "a black beard," the second cyclist is a dark, cloaked figure, with no visible human features. From the opening, with its successful creation of terror in broad daylight, the viewer is hooked. (For contrast, watch the opening of the Jeremy Brett version of "The Solitary Cyclist," which may leave you intrigued, but not spooked.)

By the way, while it is sometimes easier to build upon or improve another's storyline (for example, the film adaptation of *Death On The Nile*, with Peter Ustinov as Poirot, is an improvement on the book, conflating certain minor characters and streamlining the plot while maintaining the central gimmick of misdirection), that is not always the case; and Pirie deserves credit for his picking and choosing elements from the Canon that serve the story he wants to tell.

The idea of an attractive woman stalked by a disguised man is used as a starting point by Pirie, but the various suitors of Heather Grace are not cartoonish buffoons like Woodley, who practically wears a sign announcing that he is connected to whatever plot is aimed against Violet Smith; and Grace herself is not as straightforward as the simple Violet Smith character, or, indeed, most Doyle heroines or women not named Irene Adler; she has, like Doyle, a trauma in her past and still bears the scars from it. And the simple addition of a scene in which Doyle unsuccessfully stakes out the path, seeing no one but Grace riding past, elevates the tension, and allows the viewer to entertain the possibility, despite the opening scene, that her follower is a figment of her imagination.

But while "The Solitary Cyclist" is the most obvious Canonical inspiration for major plot elements, it was not the crucial one for Pirie. Although that story contained the "arresting images in Doyle's canon," he sought to provide a framework; and "The Speckled Band" was the emotional starting point. "The Patient's Eyes" borrows some superficial aspects from "The Speckled Band," by modeling Grace's guardian Blythe, with his curious menagerie, on Dr. Grimesby Roylott, (the novel even includes a poker-bending scene omitted from the screenplay); the parallels run deeper. Both feature a woman in danger, a cruel guardian, and a perplexing mystery. In keeping with Pirie's aim to do more than create a faithful pastiche, those plot points are only the springboard for a much more complex look into the human capacity for cruelty, violence, and evil.

The writing is bolstered by the acting. Richardson does his best work as Bell in "The Patient's Eyes," aided by a script that gives him a wide range of emotions to utilize. While many Holmesians (although not I, as will be argued in a future column) did not find the emotional reaction of Christopher Plummer's Holmes in *Murder By Decree* to be in character, few, if any, would take issue with a similar outburst from Bell when he confronts one of the many characters in the story whose actions have harmed others. The other episodes in the series — "The Photographer's Chair," "The Kingdom of Bones," and "The White Knight Stratagem" — were not written by Pirie; although they are not at the level of "The Patient's Eyes", they are still superior efforts, well worth watching and its a shame that more episodes were not made.

The film also benefits from Charles Edwards as Doyle; while Laing did a decent job in the first film, Edwards is a better fit for the rôle of a slightly-older Doyle, who was withdrawn emotionally from the world after the horrors he has experienced, and who finds, in Grace, a possible soul-mate. And Katie Blake is perfect as Heather Grace, conveying with subtle facial expressions so much of the inner torment that has plagued her for years, and which is exacerbated by her hooded tormentor.

"The Patient's Eyes" is that rare Holmes film that demands repeated viewing; once the solution to the mystery is known, you can go back and see how fairly, albeit subtly, the clues have been planted, and without resorting to cheap tricks. The challenge of having clues fairly before the viewer has vexed even otherwise excellent TV-whodunit shows; the first seasons of both *Murder One* and *Veronica Mars* had their capable and bright detectives learn who the killer was by stumbling upon a convenient inculpatory videotape. And if memory serves, the TV adaptation of P. D. James's *The Murder Room* changed the story to have a visual clue, rather than an auditory one, helping Dalgleish reach a solution. By contrast, Pirie cleverly plays on viewers' expectations to fool them, and in so doing, along with a natural injection of psychological depth into all the main characters, he has managed to create one of the best Sherlock Holmes films ever.   ✗

Lenny Picker, who reviews mystery and crime fiction regularly for Publishers Weekly, *lives in New York City with his wife, two sons, three daughters, and several thousand books. He can be reached at* CHTHOMPSON@ITSA.EDU.

NOTABLE HOLMESIAN PAPERBACK PASTICHES & OTHER ODDITIES

by Gary Lovisi

Most mystery fans know that the first Sherlock Holmes story, "A Study in Scarlet" was published in the 1887 issue of *Beeton's Christmas Annual,* a magazine — but few fans know that the first Sherlock Holmes book was in fact, a paperback. In 1888 the British firm of Ward Lock & Co. reprinted *A Study in Scarlet* in a very rare paperback edition. It is considered more rare even than the *Beeton's* magazine version, of which a copy sold a while back for $50,000! That paperback was the first Sherlock Holmes book. It began a long line of Holmesian publishing in softcover that continues today over 120 years later. A facsimile was published in 1993 in a 500-copy edition and that has also become collectable. Here then, is a sampling of Holmesian highlights, oddities, and rarities.

Canonical; Books By Doyle:

One of the earliest series of canonical Holmes books (collecting the original stories written by Doyle) were those published by Tauchnitz Books. Beginning around 1893 with *The Adventures of Sherlock Holmes*, this German firm specialized in reprinting books by American and British authors for expats and tourists in Continental Europe. All books were printed in English but not for sale in America or the British Empire due to copyright restrictions. They had plain text covers and are uncommon. All Tauchnitz Books by Doyle are scarce and very collectible.

"Pirates" or pirated editions also abounded since America was not then a signer of the Berne Copyright Convention — publishers did not pay foreign authors to reprint their work. One interesting American pirate edition was *A Study in Scarlet* from the Golden Gem Library, #17 from April 25, 1892, which had a plain text cover in gold lettering. A later version of the same book from the Arthur Westbrook Company of Cleveland, Ohio, was published circa 1900–1910 and had an early illustrated cover.

Pocket Books was the first American mass-market paperback outfit to reprint a collection of Holmes stories in *The Sherlock Holmes Pocket Book* (Pocket #95, 1941), a first edition collection. It was reprinted many times with the same cover art but the 11th printing in 1944 had a new cover. That variant edition is very scarce.

Bantam Books reprinted three Holmes books in mass-market paperback beginning in 1949 with *The Hound of The Baskervilles* (Bantam #366). This edition showed sexy bondage cover art by William Shoyer more in keeping with the pulp-style popular at the time than having anything to do with our Mr. Holmes. More on target was *Memoirs of Sherlock Holmes* (Bantam #704, 1949) with the cover art showing a traditional battle between Holmes and Moriarty, and *The Valley of Fear* (Bantam #733, 1950) showing Holmes and Watson.

British paperbacks also offer some wonderful cover images; editions from John Murray and Pan Books are popular with collectors. *The Valley of Fear* (Pan Book #177, 1951) has cover art by Philip Mendoza that shows Holmes and Watson reading a letter — or secret message! *The Return of Sherlock Holmes* (John Murray, 2nd printing, 1960) shows Colonel Sebastian Moran using his notorious airgun to try to assassinate Holmes in a scene from "The Adventure of the Empty House."

In 1956, the Western Publishing Company produced *Sherlock Holmes*, a nicely done collection of stories that was a giveaway from Nestles Chocolate. It also appeared in 1968 in a couple of different formats, but always with the same cover art. It has since become scarce.

Pastiches; Not By Doyle:

The pastiche is a time honored form of literature — in the style of another artist. From the earliest days of Sherlock Holmes the popularity of the Great Detective leads to a plethora of pastiche tales. In the early days, at the turn of the 20th Century, copyright restriction caused Sherlockian pastiches (and parodies) to feature detective heroes with the most unlikely names — Herlock Sholmes, Padlock Jones, Hemlock Coombs, and more. Diehard Holmesians wrote their own tales that continued the adventures, or addressed the dozens of intriguing cases mentioned by Watson in the canon, which had been left untold, or to retell existing stories in new and different ways.

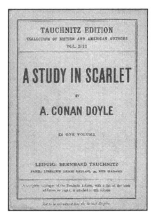

Once the copyright on the Holmes stories expired in the 1970s a floodgate was opened up, and the first book to take advantage of this new reality was Nicholas Meyer's bestseller, *The Seven Per-Cent Solution*. The book was a Dutton hardcover from 1974, but what a lot of fans and collectors don't know is that there was a rare advance reading copy published by Dutton months earlier in illustrated wraps (trade paperback size), with the same David K. Stone cave- art which would appear on the hardcover. Meyer's book really jump-started the pastiche-writing craze which has become a sub-genre, and some may say a mini-industry, all its own today.

Meyer went on to write two more Holmes pastiche novels but neither attained the success of his first. However, many more writers would step up to fill the breach, some who are well-known names in the mystery, science-fiction, fantasy and even horror fields.

Two of what I consider to be the best and most entertaining Holmes pastiches are mystery writer Richard L. Boyer's *The Giant Rat of Sumatra* (Warner Books, 1976) a paperback original and his first book — it tells a tale "for which the world is not yet prepared." Fantasy author Manly Wade Wellman (with son, Wade) offers a classic in Sherlock Holmes's *War of The Worlds* (Warner Books, 1975). This later book is made up of four connected short stories, two originally appeared in *The Magazine of Fantasy & Science Fiction,* and two were original tales, making this a first book edition and a paperback original. It tells the story of the Martian invasion of Earth after the H.G. Wells story. It is well done and great fun.

Mystery author Stuart Palmer is also known for two well-regarded and enjoyable pastiche stories in *The Adventure of the Marked Man and One Other* (Aspen Press, 1973). This slim and uncommon volume was limited to only 500 copies as are many small-press, fan-press, or scion-society items. In fact, some of these more off-trail items are limited to only 221 copies, some even under 100 copies!

Science fiction anthologist and mystery maven Kingsley Amis wrote one pastiche, and it is also well-regarded: *The Darkwater Hall Mystery*, which originally appeared in *Playboy*, May, 1978. It was reprinted in 1978 in a slim UK paperback of only 165 copies and is quite rare today; copies sell for hundreds of dollars.

Many famous team-ups appear in Holmesian pastichedom since Meyer began the trend of teaming Holmes with Sigmund Freud in *The Seven Per-Cent Solution*. In one of the rarest and most sought after items, Holmes teams up with British secret agent, James Bond! Donald Stanley's *Holmes Meets 007* (Beaune Press, 1967, UK), is a hand-sewn slim booklet published in only 222 numbered copies. It can run you a few hundred dollars, if you can find a copy!

Meanwhile *Pulptime* by P.H. Cannon (Weirdbook Press, 1984), teamed-up Holmes with real-life horror writer H.P. Lovecraft in a memorable and spooky adventure. You could not come up with two more quirky and extreme characters than Holmes and Lovecraft. Science-fiction author Philip José Farmer teamed up Holmes with another popular fictional character, Tarzan of the Apes. *The Adventure of the Peerless Peer* was originally published in a scarce and limited edition hardcover from The Aspen Press in 1974, but it is the Dell paperback reprint that made this wonderful book easily available to legions of Holmes fans at an affordable price.

Pastiches that tie-in to hit films or have become hit films are always popular. One of the earliest was *A Study in Terror* by Ellery Queen (actually written by Paul W. Fairman), a Lancer Books paperback original from 1966. This is the first and best Holmes versus Jack-the-Ripper novel, told by Watson and Queen in alternating chapters and made into a pretty good — some might say better — film than the book.

They Might Be Giants by James Goldman (Lancer Books, 1970) is a quirky film starring George C. Scott and Joanne Woodward about a judge who thinks he is Sherlock Holmes. The paperback edition — the only edition — contains stills from the film and reprints the actual film script and is rare.

The Private Life of Sherlock Holmes is a tie-in paperback to the hilarious Billy Wilder film and was written by UK Holmesians Michael and Mollie Hardwick. It novelized the Wilder and I.A.I. Diamond screenplay and appeared as a paperback original in the UK from Mayflower Books in 1970, and was also a first US edition paperback from Bantam Books also in 1970. The Bantam paperback has the added bonus of cover art by Robert McGinnis from his US poster for the film.

Marvin Kaye is a man who wears many hats as author and anthologist, and he has written one notable pastiche, *The Incredible Umbrella* (Dell Books, 1980), a first edition paperback that collects his fine stories featuring the fantastical doings of Professor J. Adrian Fillmore (Gad, what a name!). The first two were written as separate stories and appeared in magazines in the 1970s. It is good to have them all collected in one volume.

Kaye is also known for editing three outstanding anthologies of articles, pastiches, and short stories in the Holmesian genre. All three were originally published in hardcover by St. Martins Press and then reprinted by them in trade paperback.

The first is *The Game is Afoot* (1994), a gem that collects an amazing array of classic and obscure parodies and pastiches together with newer works by popular authors.

The Resurrected Holmes (1996) features all original stories, new cases for which each was ostensibly written by a classic author in that author's style. Thus we have Paula Volsky's "The Giant Rat of Sumatra" as if written by H.P. Lovecraft and Carole Buggé's "The Madness of Colonel Warburton" as if written by Dashiell Hammett. You get the idea; this one is great fun.

The Confidential Casebook of Sherlock Holmes (1998) once again offers original pastiches by major authors, this time presenting cases supposedly surpressed to avoid scandal . . . or worse. Now the truth can be told! In these three books Kaye and his contributors offer some of the most ingenious and enjoyable Holmesian pastiches.

Carole Buggé, whose fine work appears in this magazine, has also written two excellent novels published by St. Martins Press: *The Star of India* (1998) and *The Haunting of Torre Abbey* (2000). In the former we have Holmes returning to London to discover his arch nemesis Moriarty still alive, while the latter has the Great Detective investigating strange hauntings in a 12th century monastery.

One of the best kept secrets and least known of the newer pastiches is *Sherlock Holmes on The Wild Frontier* by Magda Jozsa (Book Surge, 2005), a print-on-demand trade paperback original from a talented Australian writer. Don't let the American Wild West setting put you off; this is a fine pastiche and true to Holmes and Watson.

While I've barely scratched the surface in this short article, and I'm sure we each have our own favorites, collecting Holmesian paperbacks is fascinating fun — and you never know what you might discover! ✗

Gary Lovisi is an MWA Edgar-nominated author for his own Sherlock Holmes pastiche "The Adventure of the Missing Detective." His latest book is Sherlock Holmes: The Great Detective in Paperback & Pastiche, *a survey, index and value guide with many rare and key covers shown in full color. This large-size, spiral-bound format book is available now for $50. + $5. postage from Gryphon Books, PO Box 209, Brooklyn, NY 11228. His website is* WWW.GRYPHONBOOKS.COM.

MEET NERO WOLFE: AN HOLMESIAN PERSPECTIVE

by Bob Byrne

Readers (unknowingly) said goodbye to Sherlock Holmes in 1926's "The Adventure of the Retired Colourman." Only eight years later, a new detective who would not only evoke memories of the Holmes stories but also plough new ground arrived in the (oversized) form of Nero Wolfe. The seventy-four stories, written over forty-one years, would be collectively known as the Corpus, akin to the Holmesian Canon.

For those unfamiliar with the stories, Nero Wolfe lives in a brownstone townhouse in New York City with Archie Goodwin, Fritz Brenner, and Theodore Horstmann. This is a boy's club: no girls allowed (although Archie's romantic interest, Lily Rowan, holds a special status). Wolfe's attitude towards females makes Holmes, by comparison, appear to be a "whole-souled admirer of the womankind." Quiz: Can you identify the Holmes tale that phrase is from? Answer at the article's end.

They are a self-contained unit, with Wolfe and Archie solving crimes, Fritz cooking and taking care of the household chores, and Horstmann assisting Wolfe with his hobby, the cultivation of orchids in a rooftop greenhouse. Archie often comments on the beauty of the orchids, which is a far cry from the thoughts of General Sternwood in Raymond Chandler's *The Big Sleep*: "Nasty things. Their flesh is too much like the flesh of men, and their perfume has the rotten sweetness of corruption." Po-tay-toe, po-tah-toe, I guess.

Because the characters do not age, the stories all have a comfortable familiarity about them. Also, they are set contemporary to their writing, so while in a Holmes tale it is "always 1895," the Wolfe stories feel much more like modern mysteries, even though some are over seventy years old.

The Wolfe adventures are great reads on their own merits, but the Holmesian, using those famous powers of observation, can detect elements of the Canon throughout the Corpus.

No, You Mean My Brother

Nero Wolfe bears a much stronger resemblance to Mycroft Holmes than to his more famous brother, Sherlock. Archie frequently tells us that Wolfe is lazy, and in fact his boss prefers to takes cases only when financial necessity dictates. Archie tells us that one of his most important jobs is to browbeat Wolfe into working, which is certainly indicative of the latter's attitude towards accepting clients.

Sherlock Holmes says that his brother would rather be considered wrong than to exert the necessary energy to prove himself correct. Wolfe may not quite take things that far, but he will do his utmost to avoid taking on a case. He once said, "I am not interested, not involved, and not curious." Unless forced by circumstances, that pretty much sums up Wolfe's attitude to work.

Physically, Mycroft is described by Watson as "corpulent," which means having a large, bulky body. Wolfe actually uses the word "gargantuan" to describe himself, and while his weight varies over the years, under normal circumstances it is in the neighborhood of 285 pounds. Both Wolfe and Mycroft are very large men, but with extremely agile minds. One thinks of Sidney Greenstreet's "The Fat Man" in *The Maltese Falcon*. In fact, Greenstreet actually voiced Wolfe in a series of radio plays starting in 1950.

In *Fer de Lance*, the very first story, Wolfe is unfamiliar with the sport of golf. He has some clubs brought to his office and asks the delivery boy to demonstrate them for him. After watching a powerful swing, Wolfe mutters "Ungovernable fury." Only a man who detests unnecessary physical exertion would view a simple golf swing in that vein.

Wolfe considered venturing outside the brownstone as something to be avoided in the extreme, with only three events regularly drawing him forth: voting, dining at Rustermans, (the restaurant owned by his boyhood friend Marko Vukcik), and pursuing his orchid obsession. Other sallies forth were dictated by circumstances and universally disliked. Wolfe viewed riding in a car akin to a suicide mission. One wonders how he managed to board a plane and fly to Montana in *Some Buried Caesar*.

Both Wolfe and Mycroft are men of habits. Six days a week, Wolfe takes breakfast in his room, dresses in exactly the same fashion, spends two hours in the morning and two more in the afternoon upstairs in the plant rooms, has lunch and dinner in the dining room at set times, and only deals with business matters in the office if he absolutely must. When Wolfe enters the office for the first time, he greets Archie with a "Good morning," even if they have already spoken. Fritz must not open the beer bottles he brings to Wolfe, who does it himself, using a specific bottle opener each time. Few detectives follow as rigid a daily pattern as Wolfe.

Mycroft "has his rails" and only frequents three places: his lodgings, his government office, and the Diogenes Club. Holmes wonders what upheaval could have unsettled Mycroft's habits so much to force a visit to Baker Street. He compares it to a planet leaving its orbit.

"Give me your details, and from an armchair I will return you an excellent expert opinion. But to run here and run there . . . it is not my métier." Though this was Mycroft talking to Sherlock; it could very well have been Wolfe addressing Archie. But similarities are not limited to only Mycroft.

Moriarty? No, Zeck.

Professor James Moriarty was Sherlock Holmes's great nemesis. The detective got the better of Dr. Grimesby Roylott, Charles Augustus Milverton, John Clay, and many others; but it is Moriarty who is *the* villain in the Canon.

There is only one adversary who appears in multiple stories in the Corpus, and he is clearly the most dangerous man Wolfe faces. Three times Wolfe comes into contact with Arnold Zeck, who, like Moriarty, is the head of a criminal organization. Also like Moriarty, Zeck tries to warn the detective to stay out of his business. Failing, he has Wolfe's greenhouse destroyed with a barrage of machine-gun bullets. Later, he sends a tear-gas bomb to Wolfe's office. Just as Holmes fled 221B Baker Street, Wolfe simply abandons the brownstone and goes deep undercover: Archie doesn't even know where he is.

Holmes stayed in hiding until the opportunity arose to get Moriarty's chief lieutenant, Colonel Moran. Wolfe engaged in a similar ploy, slowly, anonymously, working his way into Zeck's organization. When the timing is right, Wolfe set a trap for his foe, just as Holmes did for Moran.

War Service

During World War I, Holmes came out of retirement to go undercover and break up a German spy ring. In World War II, Nero Wolfe essentially sets aside his private practice and works for the Army. In *Booby Trap* we watch Wolfe and Archie solve a wartime industrial espionage case fraught with murder. Wolfe and the Holmes brothers are both great patriots and serve their respective countries.

Archie!

It can be argued that Sherlock Holmes would have done just fine without Watson. While the good doctor was a more than capable chronicler, Holmes could probably have completed his investigations alone. This is partially because Holmes was a very energetic and physically capable detective.

Nero Wolfe most certainly is not. Archie does all of the legwork. Well, not quite all; he does have assistance sometimes in the form of other private operatives, somewhat of a West 35th Street equivalent to the Baker Street Irregulars.

Wolfe, quite simply, does not investigate. He thinks and he issues orders. Archie is a far more capable sidekick than Watson. He is, in fact, a licensed private investigator in his own right. When Wolfe disappears as part of his campaign against Arnold Zeck, Archie sets up shop on his own and does quite well.

Archie is brave, wise-cracking, attractive to women, athletic, and tough. He is a detective in the style of Sam Spade and gumshoes in the pages of *Black Mask Magazine*. In fact, Wolfe is an intellectual detective of the Sherlock/Mycroft era, while Archie is typical of the hard-boiled genre. Thus, Rex Stout created a detective series that was characterized by the two periods of detective fiction which bookended the Golden Era of mystery stories (of which Agatha Christie is a prime example).

Perhaps it's in the Blood?

Holmesians have often speculated that there was a romantic relationship between Sherlock Holmes and Irene Adler, with several films and pastiches utilizing the premise. John Lescroart wrote a pair of novels featuring Auguste Lupa (a name with linguistic connotations of Nero Wolfe), *Son of Holmes* and *Rasputin's Revenge*. The brilliant Lupa is the offspring of Holmes and Adler. Though it is never overtly stated, it's hard not to conclude that Lupa, who heads off to America with his Swiss chef, Fritz, at the end of the second novel, becomes Nero Wolfe. In fact, it's elementary.

Now, don't get the impression that the Wolfe stories are just pale copies of the Holmes tales. Rex Stout excelled in both plot and characterization, and the Wolfe stories hold a unique and enduring place in the mystery pantheon. But Stout was a well-known fan of Sherlock Holmes, and traces of that admiration and respect for the world's first and greatest private consulting detective can be found in the Corpus.

Beyond Stout

Unlike Sherlock Holmes, Nero Wolfe is still copyright protected, so you won't find a plethora of pastiches (there's a good name for a Wolfean mystery story) for sale in bookstores and online. However, if you've worked through the Corpus a few times and want more, there are still some options out there.

Robert Goldsborough, with permission from the Stout Estate, published seven novels featuring Wolfe and Archie. Like Stout's originals, they are contemporary tales and the last book, *The Missing Chapter*, pokes fun at pastiches of popular series.

Lawrence Block created Leo Haig, star of two novels and several short stories. Haig has learned everything that he can about Nero Wolfe, who he believes to be a very real person: Rex Stout is merely a pseudonym. He lives as a shadow of Wolfe, keeping tropical fish instead of orchids, venturing out for business only when he has to and employing his own Archie, Chip Harrison, to do the legwork. Haig's dream is to be invited to dinner at Wolfe's brownstone, which is a clever bit.

H. Paul Jeffers, who includes two Sherlock Holmes titles among his list of works, wrote three books featuring Sergeant John Bogdanovic. The policeman finds himself immersed in the world of a famous fictional detective in each novel. The third, entitled *Corpus Corpus*, centers around an annual Wolfe Pack Dinner. As expected, Wolfean details abound throughout the tale.

Finally, in 2008, Loren Estleman began a series of pastiches featuring amateur private detective Claudius Lyon, whose life mission is to emulate Nero Wolfe. Lyon's Archie is an ex-convict named Arnie Woodbine, who also serves as narrator. Estleman has long been known to Sherlock Holmes fans for two pastiches, one featuring Dracula and the other Dr. Jekyll and Mr. Hyde.

Very Satisfactory

If you have only a passing acquaintance with Nero Wolfe, you would do well to read up on the Corpus. For the more visually minded mystery lover, there is also a Nero Wolfe series available on DVD. It aired on the A&E network in 2001 and 2002 and features Maury Chaykin and Timothy Hutton. Hutton, in particular, excelled, also serving as director and executive producer on the series. It is a high-quality production with an excellent jazz soundtrack and, happily, is quite faithful to the original stories.

Quiz Answer: Holmes tells Watson that he is *not* such an admirer of women in the fourth and final novel, *The Valley of Fear*.

MRS HUDSON'S HOUSEHOLD HINTS

by (Mrs) Martha Hudson

Dear Readers,

As there has been a dearth of requests for my advice, I have decided to alter the nature of my column, focusing instead upon techniques of household management thrust upon me by the unique tenancy of Mr Sherlock Holmes and his dear companion Dr John H Watson.

However, just as I was about to submit my new column, the editor surprised me by sending along the following request for advice from one of the readers. I am happy to add it as a prefatory item, together with my considered reply.

— (Mrs) Martha Hudson

Dear Mrs Hudson,

What remedies do you suggest for the common cold or, worse yet, influenza? I am a sickly soul, and I dread winter each year. Help me to ease my pains!

Sincerely,

Sickly in Singapore

Dear Sickly,

I certainly sympathize with you. One can never be too careful, especially in this damp climate of ours. No matter how often I get after Mr. Holmes, he fails to wear his rubbers out in bad weather. It's lucky for him he has such a strong constitution or he would have died from the grippe years ago.

One must attack these things in two phases: prevention and cure. Prevention is key, of course, but if that fails, then one must of course resort to applying cures.

As to prevention, I have several recipes passed onto me by my dear mother, God rest her soul. I know that garlic is antithetical to the British character, but my maternal grandfather was Italian, so my mother picked up a few ideas from him.

Consumption of large quantities of raw garlic during cold and flu season seemed to give him protection from catching anything — of course, it could have been simply that after consuming so much garlic, he never got close enough to another human being for the transfer of germs.

A second method of prevention is, oddly enough, cleanliness. I have found that if I wash my hands before and directly after a trip to the market, I am far less likely to pick up whatever disease is out and about.

As to remedies, I have several to suggest. Any hot liquid will soothe the body; and consumption of a good quality tea, very hot, is important during this period. I suggest a strong Orange Pekoe, which is Dr Watson's favourite. If you are producing large amounts of phlegm, you might want to substitute lemon for the milk — it seems to clear the sinuses better.

I find a good hot bowl of oxtail soup is quite effective in soothing sore throats; the saltier the better. Of course you may prefer a chicken or duck broth — any clear broth will do the trick. The creamy soups are not a good idea at this time; again, they thicken the mucous, which prevents speedy healing. Adequate consumption of clear liquids is essential during this time — if you can stand it, drink large quantities of water. Alcohol should be taken only in moderation.

Hot steam in general seems to be very useful in clearing away infections of the respiratory system. Heat a large pan of water to boiling, place a towel over your head, and sit over the pan, breathing in the vapours. If you add some mint or other aromatic herbs such as lavender, you will find it even more effective.

If you do indulge in spirits, I suggest elderberry wine. My mother always kept a bottle in the cupboard. If you can get fresh elderberries, you can brew your own, or make a juice by pounding and straining them.

If you suffer from a sore throat, wrap an old sock or wool scarf around your neck, and put a night cap on before retiring for the night. Also, inhaling mint is very soothing to irritated nose and throat passages. You can even chew the leaves, if you don't mind the strong taste, or place some raw leaves in your tea and inhale that whilst drinking it.

For the fever and body aches of influenza, my mother used to have us chew on willow root, which was very effective. Dr Watson has recently told me of a powder being sold to physicians; I believe it is called "aspirin powder," discovered by a German, of all things. I can't personally recommend it, but he has heard reports that it relieves both fever and pain. I distrust Germans enough that I would not necessarily credit this report.

For sleeplessness, there is of course valerian root, as well as stronger things such as laudanum and morphia, though I hesitate to recommend these, as Mr. Holmes is given to addiction, as you may know. For coughs, I use root of licorice, as well as syrup of wild cherry. A very good thing to do is mix a good Caribbean rum with sugar or honey and lemon, add hot water, and drink as fast as you can. This will calm your cough as well as help you sleep. If you don't mind the taste, fresh or powdered ginger is excellent to add as well — it seems to reduce inflammation.

Other ideas are to sip rosehips tea, suck on horehound candy, and eat roast beef with horseradish. If you like Indian food, by all means, eat some – there is something about the spices in it that seems to reduce inflammation and calm the system.

I do hope this helps a bit, and that you have a healthier winter this year.

And now here are a few of my household hints learned during Mr Holmes's occupancy:

Removal of Bloodstains from Carpet or Other Upholstery

In my capacity as Mr Holmes's landlady, I was occasionally faced with the problem of unsightly stains of various fluids on my carpets and furniture.

As some of you may know, blood, like egg yolk, is a protein, and therefore you must *never* put hot water on a bloodstain. Firstly blot off any excess blood, then treat with cold water — as quickly as you can, as stains will set the longer they are present. Once you have put plenty of cold water on the spot, combine one teaspoon laundry soap and one cup three per-cent solution of hydrogen peroxide in a small bowl. Soak a clean cloth or sponge in the mixture, squeeze it halfway dry, then gently blot the stain. Repeat as many times as necessary until the stain is gone.

Removal of Noxious Chemical Odours

Mr Holmes, God bless him, is not the most considerate of tenants, I am sorry to say. It is not an infrequent occurrence for me to enter his rooms and find myself quite overcome with a most unpleasant — and occasionally noxious — chemical smell. Indeed, at times one can see yellow fumes hanging in the air, and I have been awakened more than once in the middle of the night by the sound of an explosion upstairs.

So, for those of you plagued with either thoughtless tenants or young boys of an unfortunately curious disposition, I thought perhaps a few helpful hints might be in order.

I find the best method is of course to air out the room, if

possible. However, there are often lingering odours for days afterwards. I am a great proponent of aromatic herbs; and for chemical smells I use a combination of dried lavender, thyme, and rosemary, which are all quite pungent and will fill the room with an agreeable smell if you put dried bouquets around the room, after first waving them about as you walk through the room. If a chemical has landed unhappily on a piece of furniture or the floor, then I suggest cleaning with a solution made up of rose water with fresh leaves of mint crumpled up in it.

And now, as promised last issue, here are some of my favourite recipes.

Mrs Hudson's Finnan Haddie Sandwich

As Mr Holmes and Dr Watson are frequently on their way out when I am about to serve dinner, I have become very flexible in my ability to accommodate their unusual schedule. I often send them off with a box of sandwiches that I learned from my Scottish grandmother, God rest her soul.

For each sandwich:
- 2 slices of buttered bread
- Fresh watercress, chopped
- 1 large slice boned, cooked Finnan Haddie (sole or cod will do if you must substitute)
- 1 tablespoon mayonnaise

Mayonnaise sauce:
- 1 teaspoon of pepper
- 2 teaspoons of mustard
- 1 teaspoon of salt
- 2 egg yolks
- 2 tablespoon of vinegar
- 1 & 1/2 cups of olive oil

1. Mix mustard, pepper, and salt with egg yolks.
2. Add 1 tablespoon vinegar.
3. Gradually add 1 & 1/2 cups of olive oil, mixing constantly.
4. As soon as the mixture thickens, thin it with a little more vinegar. Proceed until the full two tablespoons of vinegar and all the oil is used. Mayonnaise should be stiff enough to hold its shape.

To make the sandwich:

Mix all ingredients together.

Spread on both slices, add fresh watercress, put together and press lightly.

Mrs Hudson's Bubble and Squeak

A nourishing breakfast for Mr Holmes and Dr Watson — a favourite of theirs on Sunday mornings.

- 1 pound Sausage meat
- 1/2 Onion, chopped
- 2 cups cooked chopped cabbage
- 1 cup chopped green pepper or watercress
  Salt to taste
- 2 cups white sauce

Directions:

Preheat oven to 350 degrees. Butter a 1–1/2-quart casserole. Cook the sausage meat in a skillet, breaking it up with a fork as it cooks. When no pink shows, transfer it to a bowl. Add the chopped onion to the sausage drippings in the skillet and cook until limp. Add to the meat and mix well.

Spread the meat on the bottom of the casserole. Cover with the cabbage and green pepper or watercress, add salt to taste, then cover with the sauce, and bake for 30–40 minutes, or until bubbling hot.

For the white sauce, mix two tablespoons butter with an equal amount of flour and cook until the flour is just beginning to brown. Add one cup good homemade chicken stock and one cup fresh milk or light cream; stir until thickened.

Mrs Hudson's Curried Lamb Shank

(which kept Mr Holmes warm on cold London nights)

- lamb shanks, 2 lamb shoulders steaks (yielding about 2 lbs of meat without the bone)
- 2 large onions, chopped
- 3–5 cloves of garlic, crushed
- 2 Tbsp ghee (clarified butter) or olive oil with butter
- 2 Tbsp curry powder — Madras or other yellow curry
- 1 tsp salt
- 1 tsp black pepper
- 1 lemon sliced (with rind)
- 2 peeled and chopped apples (tart green granny smith if possible)

- 1/2 cup of dried fruit, such as raisins of cranberries
- 1 cup of chicken or duck broth
- 8 small red potatoes, quartered
- Chutney, yogurt, rice

Marinate lamb pieces overnight in the following marinade:
- 1 Tbsp of coriander seeds
- 1 Tbsp cumin
- 1 Tbsp curry powder
- 1 tsp fresh rosemary leaves
- 1/2 tsp sage
- 1 tsp thyme
- 1/2 tsp salt
- 1/2 tsp pepper
- 2 Tbsp olive oil

Directions

Preheat oven to 300 degrees F. On stovetop, brown the marinated meat in a little bit of olive oil in an oven-safe pan. Remove meat from pan.

Add ghee (or olive oil with a bit of butter) to pan, add curry powder, cook gently for a minute or two. Add onions and garlic and cook 5 minutes. Return meat to pan.

Add sliced lemon, apples, raisins, chicken broth, salt and pepper. Put pan, covered, in oven and cook for 3 hours. In the last 45 minutes, remove from oven and put in potatoes. Return to oven. Serve with chutney and yogurt over rice. Serves 6.

Next time I will give you my recipe for Scotch eggs, a favourite of Dr Watson's. Until then, happy cooking!

THE ADVENTURE OF THE SPECKLED BAND

by Sir Arthur Conan Doyle

On glancing over my notes of the seventy-odd cases in which I have during the last eight years studied the methods of my friend Sherlock Holmes, I find many tragic, some comic, a large number merely strange, but none commonplace; for, working as he did rather for the love of his art than for the acquirement of wealth, he refused to associate himself with any investigation which did not tend towards the unusual, and even the fantastic. Of all these varied cases, however, I cannot recall any which presented more singular features than that which was associated with the well-known Surrey family of the Roylotts of Stoke Moran. The events in question occurred in the early days of my association with Holmes, when we were sharing rooms as bachelors in Baker Street. It is possible that I might have placed them upon record before, but a promise of secrecy was made at the time, from which I have only been freed during the last month by the untimely death of the lady to whom the pledge was given. It is perhaps as well that the facts should now come to light, for I have reasons to know that there are widespread rumours as to the death of Dr Grimesby Roylott which tend to make the matter even more terrible than the truth.

It was early in April in the year '83 that I woke one morning to find Sherlock Holmes standing, fully dressed, by the side of my bed. He was a late riser, as a rule, and as the clock on the mantelpiece showed me that it was only a quarter-past seven, I blinked up at him in some surprise, and perhaps just a little resentment, for I was myself regular in my habits.

"Very sorry to knock you up, Watson," said he, "but it's the common lot this morning. Mrs Hudson has been knocked up, she retorted upon me, and I on you."

"What is it, then — a fire?"

"No; a client. It seems that a young lady has arrived in a considerable state of excitement, who insists upon seeing me. She is waiting now in the sitting-room. Now, when young ladies wander about the metropolis at this hour of the morning, and knock sleepy people up out of their beds, I presume that it is something very pressing which they have to communicate. Should it prove to be an interesting case, you would, I am sure, wish to follow it from the outset. I thought, at any rate, that I should call you and give you the chance."

"My dear fellow, I would not miss it for anything."

I had no keener pleasure than in following Holmes in his professional investigations, and in admiring the rapid deductions, as swift as intuitions, and yet always founded on a logical basis with which he unravelled the problems which were submitted to him. I rapidly threw on my clothes and was ready in a few minutes to accompany my friend down to the sitting-room. A lady dressed in black and heavily veiled, who had been sitting in the window, rose as we entered.

"Good-morning, madam," said Holmes cheerily. "My name is Sherlock Holmes. This is my intimate friend and associate, Dr Watson, before whom you can speak as freely as before myself. Ha! I am glad to see that Mrs Hudson has had the good sense to light the fire. Pray draw up to it, and I shall order you a cup of hot coffee, for I observe that you are shivering."

"It is not cold which makes me shiver," said the woman in a low voice, changing her seat as requested.

"What, then?"

"It is fear, Mr Holmes. It is terror." She raised her veil as she spoke, and we could see that she was indeed in a pitiable state of agitation, her face all drawn and grey, with restless frightened eyes, like those of some hunted animal. Her features and figure were those of a woman of thirty, but her hair was shot with premature grey, and her expression was weary and haggard. Sherlock Holmes ran her over with one of his quick, all-comprehensive glances.

"You must not fear," said he soothingly, bending forward and patting her forearm. "We shall soon set matters right, I have no doubt. You have come in by train this morning, I see."

"You know me, then?"

"No, but I observe the second half of a return ticket in the palm of your left glove. You must have started early, and yet you had a good drive in a dog-cart, along heavy roads, before you reached the station."

The lady gave a violent start and stared in bewilderment at my companion.

"There is no mystery, my dear madam," said he, smiling. "The left arm of your jacket is spattered with mud in no less than seven places. The marks are perfectly fresh. There is no vehicle save a dog-cart which throws up mud in that way, and then only when you sit on the left-hand side of the driver."

"Whatever your reasons may be, you are perfectly correct," said she. "I started from home before six, reached Leatherhead at twenty past, and came in by the first train to Waterloo. Sir, I can stand this strain no longer; I shall go mad if it continues. I have no one to turn to — none, save only one, who cares for me, and he, poor fellow, can be of little aid. I have heard of you, Mr Holmes; I have heard of you from Mrs Farintosh, whom you helped in the hour of her sore need. It was from her that I had your address. Oh, sir, do you not think that you could help me, too, and at least throw a little light through the dense darkness which surrounds me? At present it is out of my power to reward you for your services, but in a month or six weeks I shall be married, with the control of my own income, and then at least you shall not find me ungrateful."

Holmes turned to his desk and, unlocking it, drew out a small case-book, which he consulted.

"Farintosh," said he. "Ah yes, I recall the case; it was concerned with an opal tiara. I think it was before your time, Watson. I can only say, madam, that I shall be happy to devote the same care to your case as I did to that of your friend. As to reward, my profession is its own reward; but you are at liberty to defray whatever expenses I may be put to, at the time which suits you best. And now I beg that you will lay before us everything that may help us in forming an opinion upon the matter."

"Alas!" replied our visitor, "the very horror of my situation lies in the fact that my fears are so vague, and my suspicions depend so entirely upon small points, which might seem trivial to another, that even he to whom of all others I have a right to look for help and advice looks upon all that I tell him about it as the fancies of a nervous woman. He does not say so, but I can read it from his soothing answers and averted eyes. But I have heard, Mr Holmes, that you can see deeply into the manifold wickedness of the human heart. You may advise me how to walk amid the dangers which encompass me."

"I am all attention, Madam."

"My name is Helen Stoner, and I am living with my stepfather, who is the last survivor of one of the oldest Saxon families in England, the Roylotts of Stoke Moran, on the western border of Surrey."

Holmes nodded his head. "The name is familiar to me," said he.

"The family was at one time among the richest in England, and the estates extended over the borders into Berkshire in the north, and Hampshire in the west. In the last century, however, four successive heirs were of a dissolute and wasteful disposition, and the family ruin was eventually completed by a gambler in the days of the Regency. Nothing was left save a few acres of ground, and the two-hundred-year-old house, which is itself crushed under a heavy mortgage. The last squire dragged out his existence there, living the horrible life of an aristocratic pauper; but his only son, my stepfather, seeing that he must adapt himself to the new conditions, obtained an advance from a relative, which enabled him to take a medical degree and went out to Calcutta, where, by his professional skill and his force of character, he established a large practice. In a fit of anger, however, caused by some robberies which had been perpetrated in the house, he beat his native butler to death and narrowly escaped a capital sentence. As it was, he suffered a long term of imprisonment and afterwards returned to England a morose and disappointed man.

"When Dr Roylott was in India he married my mother, Mrs Stoner, the young widow of Major-General Stoner, of the Bengal Artillery. My sister Julia and I were twins, and we were only two years old at the time of my mother's re-marriage. She had a considerable sum of money — not less than 1000 pounds a year — and this she bequeathed to Dr Roylott entirely while we resided with him, with a provision that a certain annual sum should be allowed to each of us in the event of our marriage. Shortly after our return to England my mother died — she was killed eight years ago in a railway accident near Crewe. Dr Roylott then abandoned his attempts to establish himself in practice in London and took us to live with him in the old ancestral house at Stoke Moran. The money which my mother had left was enough for all our wants, and there seemed to be no obstacle to our happiness.

"But a terrible change came over our stepfather about this time. Instead of making friends and exchanging visits with our neighbours, who had at first been overjoyed to see a Roylott of Stoke Moran back in the old family seat, he shut himself up in his house and seldom came out save to indulge in ferocious quarrels with whoever might cross his path. Violence of temper approaching to mania has been hereditary in the men of the family, and in my stepfather's case it had, I believe, been intensified by his long residence in the tropics. A series of disgraceful brawls took place, two of which ended in the police-court, until at last he became the terror of the village, and the folks would fly at his approach, for he is a man of immense strength, and absolutely uncontrollable in his anger.

"Last week he hurled the local blacksmith over a parapet into a stream, and it was only by paying over all the money which I could gather together that I was able to avert another public exposure. He had no friends at all save the wandering gipsies, and he would give these vagabonds leave to encamp upon the few acres of bramble-covered land which represent the family estate, and would accept in return the hospitality of their tents, wandering away with them sometimes for weeks on end. He has a passion also for Indian animals, which are sent over to him by a correspondent, and he has at this moment a cheetah and a baboon, which wander freely over his grounds and are feared by the villagers almost as much as their master.

"You can imagine from what I say that my poor sister Julia and I had no great pleasure in our lives. No servant would stay with us, and for a long time we did all the work of the house. She was but thirty at the time of her death, and yet her hair had already begun to whiten, even as mine has."

"Your sister is dead, then?"

"She died just two years ago, and it is of her death that I wish to speak to you. You can understand that, living the life which I have described, we were little likely to see anyone of our own age and position. We had, however, an aunt, my mother's maiden sister, Miss Honoria Westphail, who lives near Harrow, and we were occasionally allowed to pay short visits at this lady's house. Julia went there at Christmas two years ago, and met there a half-pay major of marines, to whom she became engaged. My stepfather learned of the engagement when my sister returned and offered no objection to the marriage; but within a fortnight of the day which had been fixed for the wedding, the terrible event occurred which has deprived me of my only companion."

Sherlock Holmes had been leaning back in his chair with his eyes closed and his head sunk in a cushion, but he half opened his lids now and glanced across at his visitor.

"Pray be precise as to details," said he.

"It is easy for me to be so, for every event of that dreadful time is seared into my memory. The manor-house is, as I have already said, very old, and only one wing is now inhabited. The bedrooms in this wing are on the ground floor, the sitting-rooms being in the central block of the buildings. Of these bedrooms the first is Dr Roylott's, the second my sister's, and the third my own. There is no communication between them, but they all open out into the same corridor. Do I make myself plain?"

"Perfectly so."

"The windows of the three rooms open out upon the lawn. That fatal night Dr Roylott had gone to his room early, though we knew that he had not retired to rest, for my sister was troubled by the smell of the strong Indian cigars which it was his custom to smoke. She left her room, therefore, and came into mine, where she sat for some time, chatting about her approaching wedding. At eleven o'clock she rose to leave me, but she paused at the door and looked back.

" 'Tell me, Helen,' said she, 'have you ever heard anyone whistle in the dead of the night?'

" 'Never,' said I.

" 'I suppose that you could not possibly whistle, yourself, in your sleep?'

" 'Certainly not. But why?'

" 'Because during the last few nights I have always, about three in the morning, heard a low, clear whistle. I am a light sleeper, and it has awakened me. I cannot tell where it came from — perhaps from the next room, perhaps from the lawn. I thought that I would just ask you whether you had heard it.' "

" 'No, I have not. It must be those wretched gipsies in the plantation.'

" 'Very likely. And yet if it were on the lawn, I wonder that you did not hear it also.'

" 'Ah, but I sleep more heavily than you.'

" 'Well, it is of no great consequence, at any rate.' She smiled back at me, closed my door, and a few moments later I heard her key turn in the lock." 'Indeed," said Holmes. "Was it your custom always to lock yourselves in at night?"

"Always."

"And why?"

"I think that I mentioned to you that the doctor kept a cheetah and a baboon. We had no feeling of security unless our doors were locked."

"Quite so. Pray proceed with your statement."

"I could not sleep that night. A vague feeling of impending misfortune impressed me. My sister and I, you will recollect, were twins, and you know how subtle are the links which bind two souls which are so closely allied. It was a wild night. The wind was howling outside, and the rain was beating and splashing against the windows. Suddenly, amid all the hubbub of the gale, there burst forth the wild scream of a terrified woman. I knew that it was my sister's voice. I sprang from my bed, wrapped a shawl round me, and rushed into the corridor. As I opened my door I seemed to hear a low whistle, such as my sister described, and a few moments later a clanging sound, as if a mass of metal had fallen. As I ran down the passage, my sister's door was unlocked, and revolved slowly upon its hinges. I stared at it horror-stricken, not knowing what was about to issue from it. By the light of the corridor-lamp I saw my sister appear at the opening, her face blanched with terror, her hands groping for help, her whole figure swaying to and fro like that of a drunkard. I ran to her and threw my arms round her, but at that moment her knees seemed to give way and she fell to the ground. She writhed as one who is in terrible pain, and her limbs were dreadfully convulsed. At first I thought that she had not recognised me, but as I bent over her she suddenly shrieked out in a voice which I shall never forget, 'Oh, my God! Helen! It was the band! The speckled band!' There was something else which she would fain have said, and she stabbed with her finger into the air in the direction of the doctor's room, but a fresh convulsion seized her and choked her words. I rushed out, calling loudly for my stepfather, and I met him hastening from his room in his dressing-gown. When he reached my sister's side she was unconscious, and though he poured brandy down her throat and sent for medical aid from the village, all efforts were in vain, for she slowly sank and died without having recovered her consciousness. Such was the dreadful end of my beloved sister."

"One moment," said Holmes, "are you sure about this whistle and metallic sound? Could you swear to it?"

"That was what the county coroner asked me at the inquiry. It is my strong impression that I heard it, and yet, among the crash of the gale and the creaking of an old house, I may possibly have been deceived."

"Was your sister dressed?"

"No, she was in her night-dress. In her right hand was found the charred stump of a match, and in her left a match-box."

"Showing that she had struck a light and looked about her when the alarm took place. That is important. And what conclusions did the coroner come to?"

"He investigated the case with great care, for Dr Roylott's conduct had long been notorious in the county, but he was unable to find any satisfactory cause of death. My evidence showed that the door had been fastened upon the inner side, and the windows were blocked by old-fashioned shutters with broad iron bars, which were secured every night. The walls were carefully sounded, and were shown to be quite solid all round, and the flooring was also thoroughly examined, with the same result. The chimney is wide, but is barred up by four large staples. It is certain, therefore, that my sister was quite alone when she met her end. Besides, there were no marks of any violence upon her."

"How about poison?"

"The doctors examined her for it, but without success."

"What do you think that this unfortunate lady died of, then?"

"It is my belief that she died of pure fear and nervous shock, though what it was that frightened her I cannot imagine."

"Were there gipsies in the plantation at the time?"

"Yes, there are nearly always some there."

"Ah, and what did you gather from this allusion to a band — a speckled band?"

"Sometimes I have thought that it was merely the wild talk of delirium, sometimes that it may have referred to some band of people, perhaps to these very gipsies in the plantation. I do not know whether the spotted handkerchiefs which so many of them wear over their heads might have suggested the strange adjective which she used."

Holmes shook his head like a man who is far from being satisfied.

"These are very deep waters," said he; "pray go on with your narrative."

"Two years have passed since then, and my life has been until lately lonelier than ever. A month ago, however, a dear friend, whom I have known for many years, has done me the honour to ask my hand in marriage. His name is Armitage — Percy Armitage — the second son of Mr Armitage, of Crane Water, near Reading. My stepfather has offered no opposition to the match, and we are to be married in the course of the spring. Two days ago some repairs were started in the west wing of the building, and my bedroom wall has been pierced, so that I have had to move into the chamber in which my sister died, and to sleep in the very bed in which she slept. Imagine, then, my thrill of terror when last night, as I lay awake, thinking over her terrible fate, I suddenly heard in the silence of the night the low whistle which had been the herald of her own death. I sprang up and lit the lamp, but nothing was to be seen in the room. I was too shaken to go to bed again, however, so I dressed, and as soon as it was daylight I slipped down, got a dog-cart at the Crown Inn, which is opposite, and drove to Leatherhead, from whence I have come on this morning with the one object of seeing you and asking your advice."

"You have done wisely," said my friend. "But have you told me all?"

"Yes, all."

"Miss Roylott, you have not. You are screening your stepfather."

"Why, what do you mean?"

For answer Holmes pushed back the frill of black lace which fringed the hand that lay upon our visitor's knee. Five little livid spots, the marks of four fingers and a thumb, were printed upon the white wrist.

"You have been cruelly used," said Holmes.

The lady coloured deeply and covered over her injured wrist. "He is a hard man," she said, "and perhaps he hardly knows his own strength."

There was a long silence, during which Holmes leaned his chin upon his hands and stared into the crackling fire.

"This is a very deep business," he said at last. "There are a thousand details which I should desire to know before I decide upon our course of action. Yet we have not a moment to lose. If we were to come to Stoke Moran to-day, would it be possible for us to see over these rooms without the knowledge of your stepfather?"

"As it happens, he spoke of coming into town to-day upon some most important business. It is probable that he will be away all day, and that there would be nothing to disturb you. We have a housekeeper now, but she is old and foolish, and I could easily get her out of the way."

"Excellent. You are not averse to this trip, Watson?"

"By no means."

"Then we shall both come. What are you going to do yourself?"

"I have one or two things which I would wish to do now that I am in town. But I shall return by the twelve o'clock train, so as to be there in time for your coming."

"And you may expect us early in the afternoon. I have myself some small business matters to attend to. Will you not wait and breakfast?"

"No, I must go. My heart is lightened already since I have confided my trouble to you. I shall look forward to seeing you again this afternoon." She dropped her thick black veil over her face and glided from the room.

"And what do you think of it all, Watson?" asked Sherlock Holmes, leaning back in his chair.

"It seems to me to be a most dark and sinister business."

"Dark enough and sinister enough."

"Yet if the lady is correct in saying that the flooring and walls are sound, and that the door, window, and chimney are impassable, then her sister must have been undoubtedly alone when she met her mysterious end."

"What becomes, then, of these nocturnal whistles, and what of the very peculiar words of the dying woman?"

"I cannot think."

"When you combine the ideas of whistles at night, the presence of a band of gipsies who are on intimate terms with this old doctor, the fact that we have every reason to believe that the doctor has an interest in preventing his stepdaughter's marriage, the dying allusion to a band, and, finally, the fact that Miss Helen Stoner heard a metallic clang, which might have been caused by one of those metal bars that secured the shutters falling back into its place, I think that there is good ground to think that the mystery may be cleared along those lines."

"But what, then, did the gipsies do?"

"I cannot imagine."

"I see many objections to any such theory."

"And so do I. It is precisely for that reason that we are going to Stoke Moran this day. I want to see whether the objections are fatal, or if they may be explained away. But what in the name of the devil!"

The ejaculation had been drawn from my companion by the fact that our door had been suddenly dashed open, and that a huge man had framed himself in the aperture. His costume was a peculiar mixture of the professional and of the agricultural, having a black top-hat, a long frock-coat, and a pair of high gaiters, with a hunting-crop swinging in his hand. So tall was he that his hat actually brushed the cross bar of the doorway, and his breadth seemed to span it across from side to side. A large face, seared with a thousand wrinkles, burned yellow with the sun, and marked with every evil passion, was turned from one to the other of us, while his deep-set, bile-shot eyes, and his high, thin, fleshless nose, gave him somewhat the resemblance to a fierce old bird of prey.

"Which of you is Holmes?" asked this apparition.

"My name, sir; but you have the advantage of me," said my companion quietly.

"I am Dr Grimesby Roylott, of Stoke Moran."

"Indeed, Doctor," said Holmes blandly. "Pray take a seat."

"I will do nothing of the kind. My stepdaughter has been here. I have traced her. What has she been saying to you?"

"It is a little cold for the time of the year," said Holmes.

"What has she been saying to you?" screamed the old man furiously.

"But I have heard that the crocuses promise well," continued my companion imperturbably.

"Ha! You put me off, do you?" said our new visitor, taking a step forward and shaking his hunting-crop. "I know you, you scoundrel! I have heard of you before. You are Holmes, the meddler."

My friend smiled.

"Holmes, the busybody!"

His smile broadened.

"Holmes, the Scotland Yard Jack-in-office!"

Holmes chuckled heartily. "Your conversation is most entertaining," said he. "When you go out close the door, for there is a decided draught."

"I will go when I have said my say. Don't you dare to meddle with my affairs. I know that Miss Stoner has been here. I traced her! I am a dangerous man to fall foul of! See here." He stepped swiftly forward, seized the poker, and bent it into a curve with his huge brown hands.

"See that you keep yourself out of my grip," he snarled, and hurling the twisted poker into the fireplace he strode out of the room.

"He seems a very amiable person," said Holmes, laughing. "I am not quite so bulky, but if he had remained I might have shown him that my grip was not much more feeble than his own." As he spoke he picked up the steel poker and, with a sudden effort, straightened it out again.

"Fancy his having the insolence to confound me with the official detective force! This incident gives zest to our investigation, however, and I only trust that our little friend will not suffer from her imprudence in allowing this brute to trace her. And now, Watson, we shall order breakfast, and afterwards I shall walk down to Doctors' Commons, where I hope to get some data which may help us in this matter."

It was nearly one o'clock when Sherlock Holmes returned from his excursion. He held in his hand a sheet of blue paper, scrawled over with notes and figures.

"I have seen the will of the deceased wife," said he. "To determine its exact meaning I have been obliged to work out the present prices of the investments with which it is concerned. The total income, which at the time of the wife's death was little short of 1100 pounds, is now, through the fall in agricultural prices, not more than 750 pounds. Each daughter can claim an income of 250 pounds, in case of marriage. It is evident, therefore, that if both girls had married, this beauty would have had a mere pittance, while even one of them would cripple him to a very serious extent. My morning's work has not been wasted, since it has proved that he has the very strongest motives for standing in the way of anything of the sort.

And now, Watson, this is too serious for dawdling, especially as the old man is aware that we are interesting ourselves in his affairs; so if you are ready, we shall call a cab and drive to Waterloo. I should be very much obliged if you would slip your revolver into your pocket. An Eley's No. 2 is an excellent argument with gentlemen who can twist steel pokers into knots. That and a tooth-brush are, I think, all that we need."

At Waterloo we were fortunate in catching a train for Leatherhead, where we hired a trap at the station inn and drove for four or five miles through the lovely Surrey lanes. It was a perfect day, with a bright sun and a few fleecy clouds in the heavens. The trees and wayside hedges were just throwing out their first green shoots, and the air was full of the pleasant smell of the moist earth. To me at least there was a strange contrast between the sweet promise of the spring and this sinister quest upon which we were engaged. My companion sat in the front of the trap, his arms folded, his hat pulled down over his eyes, and his chin sunk upon his breast, buried in the deepest thought. Suddenly, however, he started, tapped me on the shoulder, and pointed over the meadows.

"Look there!" said he.

A heavily timbered park stretched up in a gentle slope, thickening into a grove at the highest point. From amid the branches there jutted out the grey gables and high roof-tree of a very old mansion.

"Stoke Moran?" said he.

"Yes, sir, that be the house of Dr Grimesby Roylott," remarked the driver.

"There is some building going on there," said Holmes; "that is where we are going."

"There's the village," said the driver, pointing to a cluster of roofs some distance to the left; "but if you want to get to the house, you'll find it shorter to get over this stile, and so by the foot-path over the fields. There it is, where the lady is walking."

"And the lady, I fancy, is Miss Stoner," observed Holmes, shading his eyes. "Yes, I think we had better do as you suggest."

We got off, paid our fare, and the trap rattled back on its way to Leatherhead.

"I thought it as well," said Holmes as we climbed the stile, "that this fellow should think we had come here as architects, or on some definite business. It may stop his gossip. Good-afternoon, Miss Stoner. You see that we have been as good as our word."

Our client of the morning had hurried forward to meet us with a face which spoke her joy. "I have been waiting so eagerly for you," she cried, shaking hands with us warmly. "All has turned out splendidly. Dr Roylott has gone to town, and it is unlikely that he will be back before evening."

"We have had the pleasure of making the doctor's acquaintance," said Holmes, and in a few words he sketched out what had occurred. Miss Stoner turned white to the lips as she listened.

"Good heavens!" she cried, "he has followed me, then."

"So it appears."

"He is so cunning that I never know when I am safe from him. What will he say when he returns?"

"He must guard himself, for he may find that there is someone more cunning than himself upon his track. You must lock yourself up from him to-night. If he is violent, we shall take you away to your aunt's at Harrow. Now, we must make the best use of our time, so kindly take us at once to the rooms which we are to examine."

The building was of grey, lichen-blotched stone, with a high central portion and two curving wings, like the claws of a crab, thrown out on each side. In one of these wings the windows were broken and blocked with wooden boards, while the roof was partly caved in, a picture of ruin. The central portion was in little better repair, but the right-hand block was comparatively modern, and the blinds in the windows, with the blue smoke curling up from the chimneys, showed that this was where the family resided. Some scaffolding had been erected against the end wall, and the stone-work had been broken into, but there were no signs of any workmen at the moment of our visit. Holmes walked slowly up and down the ill-trimmed lawn and examined with deep attention the outsides of the windows.

"This, I take it, belongs to the room in which you used to sleep, the centre one to your sister's, and the one next to the main building to Dr Roylott's chamber?"

"Exactly so. But I am now sleeping in the middle one."

"Pending the alterations, as I understand. By the way, there does not seem to be any very pressing need for repairs at that end wall."

"There were none. I believe that it was an excuse to move me from my room."

"Ah! that is suggestive. Now, on the other side of this narrow wing runs the corridor from which these three rooms open. There are windows in it, of course?"

"Yes, but very small ones. Too narrow for anyone to pass through."

"As you both locked your doors at night, your rooms were unapproachable from that side. Now, would you have the kindness to go into your room and bar your shutters?"

Miss Stoner did so, and Holmes, after a careful examination through the open window, endeavoured in every way to force the shutter open, but without success. There was no slit through which a knife could be passed to raise the bar. Then with his lens he tested the hinges, but they were of solid iron, built firmly into the massive masonry. "Hum!" said he, scratching his chin in some perplexity, "my theory certainly presents some difficulties. No one could pass these shutters if they were bolted. Well, we shall see if the inside throws any light upon the matter."

A small side door led into the whitewashed corridor from which the three bedrooms opened. Holmes refused to examine the third chamber, so we passed at once to the second, that in which Miss Stoner was now sleeping, and in which her sister had met with her fate. It was a homely little room, with a low ceiling and a gaping fireplace, after the fashion of old country-houses. A brown chest of drawers stood in one corner, a narrow white-counterpaned bed in another, and a dressing-table on the left-hand side of the window. These articles, with two small wicker-work chairs, made up all the furniture in the room save for a square of Wilton carpet in the centre. The boards round and the panelling of the walls were of brown, worm-eaten oak, so old and discoloured that it may have dated from the original building of the house. Holmes drew one of the chairs into a corner and sat silent, while his eyes travelled round and round and up and down, taking in every detail of the apartment.

"Where does that bell communicate with?" he asked at last pointing to a thick bell-rope which hung down beside the bed, the tassel actually lying upon the pillow.

"It goes to the housekeeper's room."

"It looks newer than the other things?"

"Yes, it was only put there a couple of years ago."

"Your sister asked for it, I suppose?"

"No, I never heard of her using it. We used always to get what we wanted for ourselves."

"Indeed, it seemed unnecessary to put so nice a bell-pull there. You will excuse me for a few minutes while I satisfy myself as to this floor." He threw himself down upon his face with his lens in his hand and crawled swiftly backward and forward, examining minutely the cracks between the boards. Then he did the same with the wood-work with which the chamber was panelled. Finally he walked over to the bed and spent some time in staring at it and in running his eye up and down the wall. Finally he took the bell-rope in his hand and gave it a brisk tug.

"Why, it's a dummy," said he.

"Won't it ring?"

"No, it is not even attached to a wire. This is very interesting. You can see now that it is fastened to a hook just above where the little opening for the ventilator is."

"How very absurd! I never noticed that before."

"Very strange!" muttered Holmes, pulling at the rope. "There are one or two very singular points about this room. For example, what a fool a builder must be to open a ventilator into another room, when, with the same trouble, he might have communicated with the outside air!"

"That is also quite modern," said the lady.

"Done about the same time as the bell-rope?" remarked Holmes.

"Yes, there were several little changes carried out about that time."

"They seem to have been of a most interesting character — dummy bell-ropes, and ventilators which do not ventilate. With your permission, Miss Stoner, we shall now carry our researches into the inner apartment."

Dr Grimesby Roylott's chamber was larger than that of his step-daughter, but was as plainly furnished. A camp-bed, a small wooden shelf full of books, mostly of a technical character, an armchair beside the bed, a plain wooden chair against the wall, a round table, and a large iron safe were the principal things which met the eye. Holmes walked slowly round and examined each and all of them with the keenest interest.

"What's in here?" he asked, tapping the safe.

"My stepfather's business papers."

"Oh! you have seen inside, then?"

"Only once, some years ago. I remember that it was full of papers."

"There isn't a cat in it, for example?"

"No. What a strange idea!"

"Well, look at this!" He took up a small saucer of milk which stood on the top of it.

"No; we don't keep a cat. But there is a cheetah and a baboon."

"Ah, yes, of course! Well, a cheetah is just a big cat, and yet a saucer of milk does not go very far in satisfying its wants, I daresay. There is one point which I should wish to determine." He squatted down in front of the wooden chair and examined the seat of it with the greatest attention.

"Thank you. That is quite settled," said he, rising and putting his lens in his pocket. "Hullo! Here is something interesting!"

The object which had caught his eye was a small dog leash hung on one corner of the bed. The leash, however, was curled upon itself and tied so as to make a loop of whipcord.

"What do you make of that, Watson?"

"It's a common enough leash. But I don't know why it should be tied."

"That is not quite so common, is it? Ah, me! it's a wicked world, and when a clever man turns his brains to crime it is the worst of all. I think that I have seen enough now, Miss Stoner, and with your permission we shall walk out upon the lawn."

I had never seen my friend's face so grim or his brow so dark as it was when we turned from the scene of this investigation. We had walked several times up and down the lawn, neither Miss Stoner nor myself liking to break in upon his thoughts before he roused himself from his reverie.

"It is very essential, Miss Stoner," said he, "that you should absolutely follow my advice in every respect."

"I shall most certainly do so."

"The matter is too serious for any hesitation. Your life may depend upon your compliance."

"I assure you that I am in your hands."

"In the first place, both my friend and I must spend the night in your room."

Both Miss Stoner and I gazed at him in astonishment.

"Yes, it must be so. Let me explain. I believe that that is the village inn over there?"

"Yes, that is the Crown."

"Very good. Your windows would be visible from there?"

"Certainly."

"You must confine yourself to your room, on pretence of a headache, when your stepfather comes back. Then when you hear him retire for the night, you must open the shutters of your window, undo the hasp, put your lamp there as a signal to us, and then withdraw quietly with everything which you are likely to want into the room which you used to occupy. I have no doubt that, in spite of the repairs, you could manage there for one night."

"Oh, yes, easily."

"The rest you will leave in our hands."

"But what will you do?"

"We shall spend the night in your room, and we shall investigate the cause of this noise which has disturbed you."

"I believe, Mr Holmes, that you have already made up your mind," said Miss Stoner, laying her hand upon my companion's sleeve.

"Perhaps I have."

"Then, for pity's sake, tell me what was the cause of my sister's death."

"I should prefer to have clearer proofs before I speak."

"You can at least tell me whether my own thought is correct, and if she died from some sudden fright."

"No, I do not think so. I think that there was probably some more tangible cause. And now, Miss Stoner, we must leave you for if Dr Roylott returned and saw us our journey would be in vain. Good-bye, and be brave, for if you will do what I have told you, you may rest assured that we shall soon drive away the dangers that threaten you."

Sherlock Holmes and I had no difficulty in engaging a bedroom and sitting-room at the Crown Inn. They were on the upper floor, and from our window we could command a view of the avenue gate, and of the inhabited wing of Stoke Moran Manor House. At dusk we saw Dr Grimesby Roylott drive past, his huge form looming up beside the little figure of the lad who drove him. The boy had some slight difficulty in undoing the heavy iron gates, and we heard the hoarse roar of the doctor's voice and saw the fury with which he shook his clenched fists at him. The trap drove on, and a few minutes later we saw a sudden light spring up among the trees as the lamp was lit in one of the sitting-rooms.

"Do you know, Watson," said Holmes as we sat together in the gathering darkness, "I have really some scruples as to taking you to-night. There is a distinct element of danger."

"Can I be of assistance?"

"Your presence might be invaluable."

"Then I shall certainly come."

"It is very kind of you."

"You speak of danger. You have evidently seen more in these rooms than was visible to me."

"No, but I fancy that I may have deduced a little more. I imagine that you saw all that I did."

"I saw nothing remarkable save the bell-rope, and what

purpose that could answer I confess is more than I can imagine."

"You saw the ventilator, too?"

"Yes, but I do not think that it is such a very unusual thing to have a small opening between two rooms. It was so small that a rat could hardly pass through."

"I knew that we should find a ventilator before ever we came to Stoke Moran."

"My dear Holmes!"

"Oh, yes, I did. You remember in her statement she said that her sister could smell Dr Roylott's cigar. Now, of course that suggested at once that there must be a communication between the two rooms. It could only be a small one, or it would have been remarked upon at the coroner's inquiry. I deduced a ventilator."

"But what harm can there be in that?"

"Well, there is at least a curious coincidence of dates. A ventilator is made, a cord is hung, and a lady who sleeps in the bed dies. Does not that strike you?"

"I cannot as yet see any connection."

"Did you observe anything very peculiar about that bed?"

"No."

"It was clamped to the floor. Did you ever see a bed fastened like that before?"

"I cannot say that I have."

"The lady could not move her bed. It must always be in the same relative position to the ventilator and to the rope — or so we may call it, since it was clearly never meant for a bell-pull."

"Holmes," I cried, "I seem to see dimly what you are hinting at. We are only just in time to prevent some subtle and horrible crime."

"Subtle enough and horrible enough. When a doctor does go wrong he is the first of criminals. He has nerve and he has knowledge. Palmer and Pritchard were among the heads of their profession. This man strikes even deeper, but I think, Watson, that we shall be able to strike deeper still. But we shall have horrors enough before the night is over; for goodness' sake let us have a quiet pipe and turn our minds for a few hours to something more cheerful."

About nine o'clock the light among the trees was extinguished, and all was dark in the direction of the Manor House. Two hours passed slowly away, and then, suddenly, just at the stroke of eleven, a single bright light shone out right in front of us.

"That is our signal," said Holmes, springing to his feet; "it comes from the middle window."

As we passed out he exchanged a few words with the landlord, explaining that we were going on a late visit to an acquaintance, and that it was possible that we might spend the night there. A moment later we were out on the dark road, a chill wind blowing in our faces, and one yellow light twinkling in front of us through the gloom to guide us on our sombre errand.

There was little difficulty in entering the grounds, for unrepaired breaches gaped in the old park wall. Making our way among the trees, we reached the lawn, crossed it, and were about to enter through the window when out from a clump of laurel bushes there darted what seemed to be a hideous and distorted child, who threw itself upon the grass with writhing limbs and then ran swiftly across the lawn into the darkness.

"My God!" I whispered; "did you see it?"

Holmes was for the moment as startled as I. His hand closed like a vice upon my wrist in his agitation. Then he broke into a low laugh and put his lips to my ear.

"It is a nice household," he murmured. "That is the baboon."

I had forgotten the strange pets which the doctor affected. There was a cheetah, too; perhaps we might find it upon our shoulders at any moment. I confess that I felt easier in my mind when, after following Holmes's example and slipping off my shoes, I found myself inside the bedroom. My companion noiselessly closed the shutters, moved the lamp onto the table, and cast his eyes round the room. All was as we had seen it in the daytime. Then creeping up to me and making a trumpet of his hand, he whispered into my ear again so gently that it was all that I could do to distinguish the words:

"The least sound would be fatal to our plans."

I nodded to show that I had heard.

"We must sit without light. He would see it through the ventilator."

I nodded again.

"Do not go asleep; your very life may depend upon it. Have your pistol ready in case we should need it. I will sit on the side of the bed, and you in that chair."

I took out my revolver and laid it on the corner of the table.

Holmes had brought up a long thin cane, and this he placed upon the bed beside him. By it he laid the box of matches and the stump of a candle. Then he turned down the lamp, and we were left in darkness.

How shall I ever forget that dreadful vigil? I could not hear a sound, not even the drawing of a breath, and yet I knew that my companion sat open-eyed, within a few feet of me, in the same state of nervous tension in which I was myself. The shutters cut off the least ray of light, and we waited in absolute darkness.

From outside came the occasional cry of a night-bird, and once at our very window a long drawn catlike whine, which told us that the cheetah was indeed at liberty. Far away we could hear the deep tones of the parish clock, which boomed out every quarter of an hour. How long they seemed, those quarters! Twelve struck, and one and two and three, and still we sat waiting silently for whatever might befall.

Suddenly there was the momentary gleam of a light up in the direction of the ventilator, which vanished immediately, but was succeeded by a strong smell of burning oil and heated metal. Someone in the next room had lit a dark-lantern. I heard a gentle sound of movement, and then all was silent once more, though the smell grew stronger. For half an hour I sat with straining ears. Then suddenly another sound became audible — a very gentle, soothing sound, like that of a small jet of steam escaping continually from a kettle. The instant that we heard it, Holmes sprang from the bed, struck a match, and lashed furiously with his cane at the bell-pull.

"You see it, Watson?" he yelled. "You see it?"

But I saw nothing. At the moment when Holmes struck the light I heard a low, clear whistle, but the sudden glare flashing into my weary eyes made it impossible for me to tell what it was at which my friend lashed so savagely. I could, however, see that his face was deadly pale and filled with horror and loathing. He had ceased to strike and was gazing up at the ventilator when suddenly there broke from the silence of the night the most horrible cry to which I have ever listened. It swelled up louder and louder, a hoarse yell of pain and fear and anger all mingled in the one dreadful shriek. They say that away down in the village, and even in the distant parsonage, that cry raised the sleepers from their beds. It struck cold to our hearts, and I stood gazing at Holmes, and he at me, until the last echoes of it had died away into the silence from which it rose.

"What can it mean?" I gasped.

"It means that it is all over," Holmes answered. "And perhaps, after all, it is for the best. Take your pistol, and we will enter Dr Roylott's room."

With a grave face he lit the lamp and led the way down the corridor. Twice he struck at the chamber door without any reply from within. Then he turned the handle and entered, I at his heels, with the cocked pistol in my hand.

It was a singular sight which met our eyes. On the table stood a dark-lantern with the shutter half open, throwing a brilliant beam of light upon the iron safe, the door of which was ajar. Beside this table, on the wooden chair, sat Dr Grimesby Roylott clad in a long grey dressing-gown, his bare ankles protruding beneath, and his feet thrust into red heelless Turkish slippers. Across his lap lay the short stock with the long leash which we had noticed during the day. His chin was cocked upward and his eyes were fixed in a dreadful, rigid stare at the corner of the ceiling. Round his brow he had a peculiar yellow band, with brownish speckles, which seemed to be bound tightly round his head. As we entered he made neither sound nor motion.

"The band! the speckled band!" whispered Holmes.

I took a step forward. In an instant his strange headgear began to move, and there reared itself from among his hair the squat diamond-shaped head and puffed neck of a loathsome serpent.

"It is a swamp adder!" cried Holmes; "the deadliest snake in India. He has died within ten seconds of being bitten. Violence does, in truth, recoil upon the violent, and the schemer falls into the pit which he digs for another. Let us thrust this creature back into its den, and we can then remove Miss Stoner to some place of shelter and let the county police know what has happened."

As he spoke he drew the dog-leash swiftly from the dead man's lap, and throwing the noose round the reptile's neck he drew it from its horrid perch and, carrying it at arm's length, threw it into the iron safe, which he closed upon it.

Such are the true facts of the death of Dr Grimesby Roylott, of Stoke Moran. It is not necessary that I should prolong a narrative which has already run to too great a length by telling how we broke the sad news to the terrified girl, how we conveyed her by the morning train to the care of her good aunt at Harrow, of how the slow process of official inquiry came to the conclusion that the doctor met his fate while indiscreetly playing with a dangerous pet. The little which I had yet to learn of the case was told me by Sherlock Holmes as we travelled back next day.

"I had," said he, "come to an entirely erroneous conclusion which shows, my dear Watson, how dangerous it always is to reason from insufficient data. The presence of the gipsies, and the use of the word 'band,' which was used by the poor girl, no doubt, to explain the appearance which she had caught a hurried glimpse of by the light of her match, were sufficient to put me upon an entirely wrong scent. I can only claim the merit that I instantly reconsidered my position when, however, it became clear to me that whatever danger threatened an occupant of the room could not come either from the window or the door. My attention was speedily drawn, as I have already remarked to you, to this ventilator, and to the bell-rope which hung down to the bed. The discovery that this was a dummy, and that the bed was clamped to the floor, instantly gave rise to the suspicion that the rope was there as a bridge for something passing through the hole and coming to the bed. The idea of a snake instantly occurred to me, and when I coupled it with my knowledge that the doctor was furnished with a supply of creatures from India, I felt that I was probably on the right track. The idea of using a form of poison which could not possibly be discovered by any chemical test was just such a one as would occur to a clever and ruthless man who had had an Eastern training. The rapidity with which such a poison would take effect would also, from his point of view, be an advantage. It would be a sharp-eyed coroner, indeed, who could distinguish the two little dark punctures which would show where the poison fangs had done their work. Then I thought of the whistle. Of course he must recall the snake before the morning light revealed it to the victim. He had trained it, probably by the use of the milk which we saw, to return to him when summoned. He would put it through this ventilator at the hour that he thought best, with the certainty that it would crawl down the rope and land on the bed. It might or might not bite the occupant, perhaps she might escape every night for a week, but sooner or later she must fall a victim.

"I had come to these conclusions before ever I had entered his room. An inspection of his chair showed me that he had been in the habit of standing on it, which of course would be necessary in order that he should reach the ventilator. The sight of the safe, the saucer of milk, and the loop of whipcord were enough to finally dispel any doubts which may have remained. The metallic clang heard by Miss Stoner was obviously caused by her stepfather hastily closing the door of his safe upon its terrible occupant. Having once made up my mind, you know the steps which I took in order to put the matter to the proof. I heard the creature hiss as I have no doubt that you did also, and I instantly lit the light and attacked it."

"With the result of driving it through the ventilator."

"And also with the result of causing it to turn upon its master at the other side. Some of the blows of my cane came home and roused its snakish temper, so that it flew upon the first person it saw. In this way I am no doubt indirectly responsible for Dr Grimesby Roylott's death, and I cannot say that it is likely to weigh very heavily upon my conscience." ✗

Watson's Wound

by Sherlock Holmes
edited with Notes by Bruce I. Kilstein

When you're wounded and left on Afghanistan's plains —
And the women come out, to cut up what remains
Then roll to yer rifle, and blow out your brains
And go to yer God like a soldier!

— Rudyard Kipling "The Young British Soldier"

It was during one of those periods of ennui, when a soaking November rain had left a damp chill over London like a pall. A lack of stimulating casework made for close company as Watson and I searched my study for a means to occupy the time. A chance glance at my colleague saved me from what, no doubt, would have been a needle-guided descent into the depths of Morpheus.

I put down the syringe and loosed the tourniquet from my arm, choosing a soothing bowl of tobacco over the seven percent solution to address the mystery that at once had my attention. Lighting the pipe, I turned to Watson, who was in the act of studying the taxidermy of a stuffed grouse mounted near the mantle. "Thinking of Afghanistan, are you?"

He turned in surprise. "As a matter of fact, I was just now recalling those days with the Sixty-sixth. How on earth could you know what I was thinking? I was just looking at this pheasant."

"Grouse," I corrected.

"Yes, grouse. But still . . . have you been studying that Mesmer fellow?"

"Mind reading? Poppycock. I glanced at you observing the bird, but as you craned your neck to inspect the rear, you winced slightly and absently touched your shoulder. As the taxidermy made you think of shooting, and the damp chill has no doubt aggravated your shoulder, your vacant stare must only mean that you were thinking of the wound you suffered at the hand of the Ghazis."

"Savages. You astound me, Holmes."

"Elementary," I murmured, pausing to think for a moment.

It was Watson's turn to be observant. "Your silence tells me there is something more to your observation."

"There may be. If you have no objection, I propose we light the hearth and take refreshment while we probe the circumstances of your wound further."

He looked perplexed, but quickly assented to the request, as the cheerful blaze, a brandy, and a tray of Mrs. Hudson's tea and scones cut the gloom that had permeated our chambers. I watched my friend through the pleasant haze of my long cherry Churchwarden as he spread marmalade over his pastry and sleeve. "What was the bullet that wounded you?" I asked.

"The Jezail, Holmes. Bloody rifles killed over a thousand of our boys at Maiwand."

"Yes, you have remarked as such many times. Pray, remind me of the circumstances. Try to leave nothing out." I settled into my chair, staring at the fire, and pressed my fingertips together as Watson recalled the battle.

He brushed crumbs from his vest and took a draught of spirits. Clearly, the memory of events caused pain beyond the purely physical. "Eighteen-eighty. After transfer from the Fifth Northumberland Fusiliers, India to Afghanistan, I soon found myself under General Burrows near Candahar. Shortly after my arrival we prepared for one of the bloodiest battles of the war. The men had little fighting experience, but we thought that our superior training would carry our two thousand troops against the larger force of Ayoob Khan's men. Our folly was not in underestimating our skill as soldiers, but in the lack of realization of what their sheer numbers could mean. They came at us with close to twenty-five thousand."

There was no doubt of that; but I thought it not best to engage in the argument that General Burrows led an untrained force from a defensive stronghold, with little reinforcement and no water in the July desert, into the open against a fanatic native force. There could be no doubt that the campaign was doomed from the outset. I thought it best not to mention this, and let Watson continue

"The battle was a bloody Hell," Watson said. "Confusion everywhere: the roar of artillery overhead, the screams, the clash of sabers, horses."

"But as I understand it, it was the rifle shot that killed the most men," I interposed.

"Quite right. We marched with twenty-four hundred. More than nine hundred were killed. One hundred seventy-five wounded. These barbarians didn't take prisoners. If it wasn't for my batman, Murray, I have no doubt that I should have been counted in the number dead. The Ghazis attacked with overwhelming numbers, using the dry riverbeds as cover. Wave after wave came over the banks. Our artillery did little to stanch the flow. We fought bravely, but I barely had time to attend the many wounded. Men were falling everywhere, and before we had time to retreat from the initial crush, we were outflanked." He waved his hands in a desperate gesture.

After he had continued on with the details of the battle for many minutes I interjected, "The Ghazis were religious fanatics, Watson. They must have fought like fiends."

"Crazed, Holmes. But they did not break our spirit. We killed fifty-five hundred of the madmen and they failed to pursue us to Candahar to finish the route."

"The retreat must have been an ordeal in itself."

"What I remember of it."

"Pray, try your best to remember. No detail may be too small." The evening was setting in quickly in the shortening days before winter. I lit a new pipe and rose to stir the ebbing fire.

"I recall the moment of the wound as vividly as if it were a day ago. I was attending the wounds of a young cavalry officer whose horse had been shot from under him, crushing his leg. I applied a tourniquet and was looking for Murray to dress and splint, when I was hit. The force of the bullet spun me around and I fell on the unfortunate patient." Watson began to perspire as he recalled the trauma.

"Do you by chance recall the patient's name?"

He thought for a moment. "Jenkins, I believe. A captain."

"Go on."

"The round, I was later to discover, struck me between the shoulder and the clavicle and sliced the subclavian artery. If it weren't for Murray's skill and loyalty, I wouldn't be here to tell this story."

I remarked that in an ironic sense, it was because of that wound, and Watson's subsequent removal to England, that we were to make acquaintance. "Perhaps that is the so-called silver lining of the situation," Watson said.

"Indeed, but we digress."

"Yes. Well, Murray dragged me off the poor captain just as our position was about to be overrun by the screaming Ghazis. Knowing we would not be taken as prisoners, he used his kerchief as an improvised bandage, plugged the wound, and guided me to a cart with the Baggage Guard. The retreat was madness equal to the battle itself. With officers fallen, many of the company fell into disarray. Litter bearers dropped wounded and ran to save themselves, animals cast off their loads, and the wounded jammed any transport they could find in hope of escaping to the rear.

"The flight was forty-five miles back toward Candahar. A torture. No water for over thirty hours. Men losing blood and more dropping from exhaustion. Murray remained by my side as long as he could but was eventually off to aid others. I am sure that my consciousness lapsed during the ordeal. I am afraid I lost track of the good man as we eventually joined Roberts's relief forces.

"I was eventually evacuated to Peshawar. The wound healed, thankfully, but the surgeons were loath to attempt to remove the bullet due to the close proximity to the artery. Blasted thing still gives me trouble on these damp days. A harsh reminder, Holmes. I soon contracted enteric fever, as did many in the camp, and so was shipped back to England where, as you well know, I have remained."

The story was tragic, a great loss for our forces, but the details as told by my friend raised some disturbing questions. The sober lens of the drawing room is often the best place to analyze the heat and strategy of former battles. "You have cherished the souvenirs, I am certain."

He gingerly removed from his breast pocket his decoration, the Roberts Star, and a scrap of cloth stained rust, which could have only been Murray's bloodstained kerchief.

"Watson, I fear there may be more to this story than you realize."

"What's this!" he started in surprise.

"I should think that we need to examine the bullet."

"A bit too late for surgery, my good man."

"There is a way, I understand, without disturbing the slug. You've no doubt read the work of Roentgen?"

"Why, yes. Yes, the chap with the X-rays. Fascinating. A dicey business, though."

"What if I told you that the bullet might be linked to a matter of national importance?"

He pondered for a moment, unsure of what to make of my sudden and strange observations. "Well, if you think so, Holmes."

"Splendid. I believe there must be a doctor at the Royal London Hospital dabbling in this new science."

"Hedley, I think it is. Met him at a medical society meeting. Experiments with all the new electronic kit."

I rang for Mrs. Hudson. She appeared in her usual fluster wanting to know why we should require her services again so soon. "You cannot be ready for supper now?"

"No, Mrs. Hudson. Be so kind as to fetch one of the boys to run a message to the telegraph office. A matter of some urgency." I wrote two messages and handed them to her along with money for the boy. "We should have our answers soon, Watson."

The next day dawned equally dank but our spirits were undampened by the weather. The responses to our telegrams came with the morning post. We hastened through breakfast and hailed a hansom on Baker Street to guide us to the first of what would be several destinations.

We soon arrived at the London Hospital and I had the cab remain in waiting. We were shown to the offices of Dr. Hedley in the department of electrotherapeutics. "Dr. Watson, Mr. Holmes, a pleasure to receive you. I so enjoy reading about your cases that I was naturally excited to learn that I could be of service in an actual investigation," Hedley said.

"You are too kind, sir," I replied. "I would think that this promising new device would one day be a valuable tool in the fight against the criminal mind. We look forward to the demonstration. The delight, I assure you, is all ours." I was surprised when he bade us to leave our outer clothes on and then led us out into the rain through the hospital gardens. We arrived at a small tin shack near the back wall.

"Not much to look at now," Hedley explained. "Safety, you know. Keeping us away from the main building for now, but someday I hope to have a whole new department of *radiology*"

We entered and found several assistants already at work on the apparatus. The thin metal wall of the building did little to ward off the chill. Watson seemed more than perturbed at stripping to the waist upon Hedley's request.

"Sorry, Dr. Watson. Best way to sit for the radiograph." An assistant positioned Watson on a stool behind a complicated machine of tubes and wires. He positioned the end of a tube near Watson's shoulder and then had him hold what must have been the photographic plate to his chest.

"I feel like the meat in a kidney pie," he mumbled.

Hedley looked up from a notebook he used to check the exposure distances and settings. "Try to hold still now, Doctor. The exposure will only take twenty-five minutes." Hedley set a timer and let the assistant perform the exposure.

Upon finishing, we escorted the chilled Watson back to Hedley's office. He rang for tea, and I explained the investigation to him over the repast. Hedley's assistant soon arrived with the radiographic plate.

Hedley held the X-ray photograph next to a lamp on his desk and we could clearly see the image of the bullet lodged in Watson's shoulder. The bones were neatly visible, but less so than the round.

"I take it, Dr. Hedley, that the bullet appears denser than the bone because the X-rays do not penetrate the metal to the degree that they do the bone."

"That is correct, Mr. Holmes. The bone also contains minerals, and we theorize that the x-ray waves or particles, we are not quite sure, penetrate to varying degrees."

"Astounding!" Watson cried. "The application of these X-rays will change the whole art of diagnosis. To think that we can now see inside the body without cutting into it. Clever. Bloody clever."

"You are most kind, Doctor. We are still refining the technique and hope to soon establish a full department of X-ray diagnostics as more becomes known."

I checked my watch, noting that we were soon due at our next rendezvous. "Watson, have you your notebook?" He replied in the affirmative. I withdrew a small draftsman's case that I had brought and removed a pair of fine calipers. "Are the actual sizes of objects on the radiograph true to life, or is there a magnifying effect when the final image is produced?" I asked Dr. Hedley.

"You will find that the image is near exact to the finest detail, allowing that there may be some blurring to the border of an object due to the effect of motion." He gestured at our example. "Dr. Watson did an admirable job of remaining still."

"Bloody near frozen," Watson mumbled.

I examined the image with my glass and the two men drew closer. "Look here, Doctors. See how the edge of the clavicle is deformed. Must be the result of fracture and then healing. And the bullet is deformed on one end. This flattening, the result of impact with the bone. The tail end, I should think, is undamaged." It was at that end that I took the measurements. "Record, Watson, that the diameter of the bullet is zero point four five inches."

Watson duly noted the measurement and we prepared to take our leave of Dr. Hedley.

"Gentlemen, I hope I have been of service to your investigation," Dr. Hedley said.

"I am not sure what we are investigating," Watson said.

"In time, Watson." I commented.

"I would be honoured," Hedley continued, "if you would accept the radiograph with my compliments."

We took the X-ray, expressed our appreciation, and headed back through a light rain to our waiting cab. The driver had been reluctant to wait but my half-crown advance insured he was our constant companion for the remainder of our errands. I instructed the driver to take us to the ministry of the Royal Army.

"The Army, Holmes?" Watson was surely intrigued by now.

I remained silent until we arrived at the ministry. We were led through a long hall adorned with regimental flags to a small side door. We entered an office to find waiting for us my brother, Mycroft, and Lord Lytton. We exchanged greetings and Watson saluted the former Viceroy of India.

"Holmes," Watson said, "your brother almost never ventures outside the confines of the Diogenes Club."

"Just a small trip from my office in Whitehall, Doctor," Mycroft said. "Sherlock cabled me with your little mystery and I thought Lord Lytton would be interested."

"Would you *please* explain this business to me, Holmes?" Watson began to sound irritated. "Is it not enough that I've been driven through the streets in this weather, made to remove my shirt and subject myself to the torrents of the cold and those X-ray beams?"

I smiled at Watson, and I must confess, I rather enjoyed keeping him in the dark. I turned to our host and said, "With your permission, Lord Lytton, I should like to review the facts." Lord Lytton nodded his assent. "Watson, you were kind enough to recall the events of your injury at Maiwand. Just before your company was overrun, you were struck with a Jezail bullet in the shoulder."

"That's correct."

"Watson, what was your position when hit by the missile?"

"Why, I had turned from my patient to find the help of an orderly."

"And from which direction was the Ghazi advance?"

"They flanked us from the northeast and the northwest."

"But when you turned for the orderly . . ."

"I was turned toward the rear of our lines."

"Exactly! *Away* from the advancing attack. Yet you were struck from the *front* of the shoulder."

"Quite so," Watson replied.

"Therefore, Watson, we must conclude that the shot did not come from the attacking Ghazis but from the rear of your own advance."

"You mean . . ."

"You were shot by one of our own troops," Lord Lytton added gravely, and stroked his beard. There was a moment of stunned silence.

"You brought the radiograph, I see," Mycroft observed.

"Yes, I have." I held the picture to the light and briefly explained the process for the benefit of our hosts.

Mycroft immediately noted the corroborating evidence shown on the plate. "I take it, Sherlock, that you have measured the diameter of the bullet and you have recorded zero point four five inches."

Watson checked his notebook. "You are correct, Mycroft. But how could you know that? The diameter of the bullet was only just revealed moments ago by Dr. Hedley."

Mycroft looked at me in a sporting way. I shrugged. "Elementary, my dear Watson," he chuckled. "Isn't that what you say in all those stories, Sherlock?" He turned to Lord Lytton and said, "If you would be so kind." Lord Lytton selected two rifles from a long rack hung on the wall. He placed them side-by-side on a table. "Sherlock's cable was the key to confirming a suspicion we have had for some time. However, we lacked certain proof. In the confusion of battle it can be quite difficult to determine the trajectory of certain small arms fire. While it is a grim consequence of battle that men can be struck by bullets fired from their own side, one needs proof of accusations that some of these shots may be intentional."

"Subversives," Lord Lytton commented. "The blasted Indian nationalists."

"We have suspects under suspicion who could have led a subversive movement from within the ranks, yet we have lacked solid evidence," Mycroft admitted.

"Until now," I said. "You see, Watson, at the time in the battle at which you were struck there were none of the enemy at the rear of our charge." I removed the calipers from my pocket. "Here the caliper is set at zero point four five inches, the size of the bullet still lodged in your shoulder." I placed the caliper across the bore of the first rifle, the Jezail. "You see, a bullet of zero point four five caliber is too small to load in the Jezail, the rifle used by the Ghazis." I then placed the calipers across the muzzle of the second rifle. It matched exactly. "This is the Martini-Henri. It matches your bullet."

"This was the bullet fired by our own Jacobs Rifles," Mycroft said.

"Your batman, Mr. Bates . . ." Lord Lytton trailed off.

"You mean Murray?" Watson exclaimed. "He could never have shot me. He saved my life."

"No, Dr. Watson," Lytton said, "Murray was loyal to the end. He filed his reports dutifully. His last was as a witness to your shooting, implicating a Captain Reynolds. But we suspect that he was ordered from someone higher up in the nationalist movement."

"Murray was no mere orderly. He was a top informant for our side," Mycroft said.

"The subversives would keep to themselves around the regular troops, but by placing our men in inconspicuous roles, they are free to move about unnoticed, thereby gaining valuable information," Lytton added.

"Spies, Holmes, who would have guessed?" Watson said.

"Murray's position had been compromised," Mycroft said. "Sherlock's deductions would seem to confirm that the bullet that struck you was meant for Murray."

Watson looked aghast. "You see, Watson," I explained, "when you turned to call for Murray, his quick response allowed the bullet to miss him, unfortunately striking you."

"He is the true hero, then," Watson said. "I should like to thank him."

Mycroft and Lytton exchanged glances. "I am sure you can, Doctor," Mycroft said. "Your testimony will be quite helpful when we apprehend the assailant."

"You have located him, Mycroft? After so many years?" I asked.

My brother smiled at me. "There are many we keep tabs on, Sherlock. You would be surprised. Lord Lytton and I must keep a low profile on such matters, you understand. But if you and the Doctor would be so kind as to assist us, you would do our nation a service."

I turned to Watson. "Are you game, my man?"

"Anything to thank Murray," he replied.

Mycroft handed me two envelopes. "You shall have that opportunity. You will find the addresses in the envelopes." He stared hard into my eyes in silent communication.

"I understand. Thank you, gentlemen. Come, Watson, the game is afoot."

I ushered my somewhat stunned colleague to our waiting coach, nodding to acknowledge the occupants of another coach parked nearby. I opened the first envelope and instructed the driver to proceed with all speed to the next address. We dashed through the rainy streets, putting some distance between us and the coach that followed. I read the remaining portion of the document *en route.*

We arrived at a moderately sized house just west of the city. We dismounted our coach and called at the door.

A servant answered. "May I help you, gentlemen?"

"We have come to call on Captain Reynolds. Important business," I said as we entered the foyer.

"Whom shall I say is calling? The Captain is entertaining guests at tea in the library and should not be disturbed," the servant said.

I gave the man my card and told him to tell Reynolds that we were friends of Mr. Murray Bates. "He will, no doubt, wish to speak with us."

Soon, two men appeared, one in regimental attire, the other an Indian in a long coat over traditional silks. "What is the meaning of this intrusion?" Reynolds demanded.

"Captain Reynolds, we have come to inquire about Murray Bates."

Reynolds looked at his friend slyly, in silent communication. "Can't say that I know the chap."

"You will answer for his murder and the assault of my colleague, Dr. Watson." I kept my eyes fixed on the pair.

"Murder?" Watson exclaimed.

Barely had Watson time to speak when I detected a quick movement from Reynolds' silent companion. I swung my cane, deflecting the blade that the Indian deftly pulled from his sash. As he watched the knife skid over the floor, I grabbed him around the throat.

"You will unhand my friend," Reynolds said coldly as he trained a revolver on Watson.

Watson bravely stood his ground.

I maintained a firm grip on the Indian.

The crack of the pistol was near deafening in the small space.

Reynolds was knocked back in a spray of blood and glass. When the smoke cleared we found him on the floor, clutching his shoulder. Inspector Lestrade stood with his smoking gun, smiling at us through the shattered window. "Good afternoon, Mr. Holmes, Dr. Watson," he said. Lestrade's fellow officers came pouring through the front door and dragged our adversaries to a waiting wagon.

"Splendid shot, Lestrade," I remarked outside as I lit my pipe. I glanced at Watson, who was looking pale.

"Where would you boys be without us?" Lestrade asked. I handed Lestrade the warrant given to me by Lord Lytton. He glanced only briefly at the document. Lytton's seal was enough for him. He left to join his colleagues.

Our final errand of the day took us to the somber gates of Highgate Cemetery. Watson and I were all too familiar with the location, as it was the site of a dicey encounter with another bullet in our investigation of the case of "The Dead House." The address contained within Mycroft's second envelope also included the location of a gravesite. The rain was driving harder by this time and the setting of the sun somewhere behind the clouds added a darker shade to the gloomy day. Our driver took us as close to the location as the small road that wound through the headstones would provide, and we were obliged to walk a distance to our destination. Watson opened his black umbrella and I took a torch from the pocket of my overcoat to help us read the names on the stones.

"Here we are, Watson," I said. I shone the beam across a small stone to read:

Murray Bates
1859–1880
Corporal Royal Berkshires

We stared at the inscription in silence. Watson handed me the umbrella and reached into his pocket. He bent over the gravesite and unwrapped his Roberts Star from Murray's kerchief, and whispered a word of thanks as he laid the medal on the ground above Murray. The rain soaked the dried blood on the old cloth, and, for a moment, Watson's blood ran again. ✗

A VOLUME IN VERMILLION

by Kim Newman

(Being a reprint from the Reminiscences of Col. Sebastian Moran, Late of the 1st Bengalore Pioneers)

I blame that rat-weasel Stamford. He was no better at judging character than at kiting paper. Stamford later had his collar felt in Farnham, of all blasted places, and turned his fine calligrapher's hands to sewing post-bags in Dartmoor Prison. If you want to pass French government bonds, you can't afford to mix up your accents *grave* and your accents *acute* — though, as it happens, the most I picked up from Mlle Fortier, my French tutor, was an interesting, persistent itch.

Nevertheless, Archie Stamford gets no sympathy from Sebastian Moran. There's one forger they should have hanged. And, indeed, drawn, and, furthermore, quartered. Thanks to Idiot Archie, I was first drawn into the orbit, the *gravitational pull* as he would have said, of Professor James Moriarty.

In '81, I was a vigourous, if scarred, forty. I had an unrivalled bag of big cats, and a fund of stories about blasting the roaring pests. I'd stood in the Khyber Pass and faced a surge of sword-waving Pashtuns howling for British blood, potting them like grouse in season. Nothing gladdens a proper Englishman's heart — this one, at least — like the sight of a foreigner's head flying into a dozen bloody bits. I'd dangled by single-handed grip from an icy ledge in the upper Himalayas, with something huge and indistinct and furry stamping on my freezing fingers. I might not have brought home the ears and the pelt on that jaunt, but — as I promised in my article on the subject for *Tit-Bits*, 'I'll Get You, Yeti!' — there's still time for another try. I'd stood like an oak in a hurricane as Sir Augustus, the hated *pater*, spouted paragraphs of bile in my face, which boiled down to the proverbial 'cut off without a penny' business. Stuck to it, too, the mean old swine. The family loot went to a society for providing Christian undergarments to the Ashanti, with the delightful side-effect of reducing my unmarriagable sisters to boarding-house penury.

I'd taken a dagger in the lower back from a harlot in Hyderabad and a pistol-ball in the knee from the Okhrana in

Nijni-Novgorod. More to the point, I had recently been raked across the chest by the mad, wily old she-tiger the hill-heathens called "Kali's Kitten."

None of that was preparation for Moriarty!

KK got too close for the long gun, and was being playful with her jaws and paws, crunching down and swallowing my pith helmet like one of Carter's Little Liver Pills, delicately shredding my shirt with three razor-claws, digging into the skin and drawing casually across my chest. Three bloody stripes. Of course, I pulled my Webley side-arm and shot the hell-bitch through the heart. To make sure, I emptied all six chambers. After that chit in Hyderabad dirked me, I broke her nose for her; the tigress looked almost as aghast and infuriated at being killed. I wondered if girl and beast were related. I had the cat's rank breath in my face and I saw the lamps go out in her huge eyes.

One more for the trophy wall, I thought. Cat dead, Moran not: hurrah and victory!

But KK nearly murdered me after all. The stripes on my chest went septic. Good thing there's no earthly use for the male nipple, because I found myself down to just the one. Lots of grey stuff came out of me. So I was packed off back to England for proper doctoring. Since the scratches mostly cleared up on the voyage home, and all the other business similarly went away, it occurred to me that a concerted effort was made to boot me out of the sub-continent. I could think of a dozen reasons for that, and a dozen clods in stiff collars who'd be happier with me out of the picture. Maiden ladies who thought tigers out to be patted on the head and given treats. And the husbands, fathers and sweethearts of non-maiden ladies. Not to mention the old Bengalore Bastards, who didn't care to be reminded of their habit of cowering in ditches while Bloody Basher did three-fourths of their fighting for them.

Still, mustn't hold a grudge, what? Sods, the lot of them. And that's just the whites. As for the natives . . . well, let's not get started on them, shall we? We'd be here til next Tuesday.

For me, a long sea-cruise is normally an opportunity. There are always bored fellow-passengers and underworked officers knocking around with fat note-cases deep in their luggage. It's most satisfying to sit on deck playing solitaire until some booby suggests a few rounds of cards and, why just to make it *spicier*, perhaps some trifling, sixpence-a-trick element of wager. Give me two months on any ocean in the world, and I can fleece everyone aboard from the captain's lady to the bosun's second-best bum-boy, and leave each mark convinced that the ship is a nest of utter cheats with only Basher as the other honest hand in the game.

Usually, I embark *sans sou* and stroll down the gang-plank at the destination pockets a-jingle with the accumulated fortune of my fellow voyagers. I get a warm feeling from ambling through the docks, listening to clots explaining to the eager sorts who've turned up to greet them that, sadly, the moolah that would have saved the guano-grubbing business or bought the Bibles for the mission or paid for the wedding has gone astray on the high seas. This time, tragic to report, I was off sick, practically in quarantine. My nimble fingers were away from the pasteboards and employed mostly in scratching *around* the bandages while trying hard not to scratch the bandages themselves.

So, the upshot. Basher in London, out of funds. And the word was abroad, so I was politely informed by a chinless receptionist at Claridge's in Brook Street that my usual suite of rooms was engaged and that, unfortunately, no alternative was available, this being a busy wet February and all. If I hadn't pawned my horsewhip, it would have got quite a bit of use. If there's any breed I despise more than natives, it's people who work in bloody hotels. Thieves, the lot of them, or, what's worse, sneaks and snitches. They talk among themselves, so it was no use trotting down to the end of the street and trying somewhere else.

I was on the point of wondering if I shouldn't risk the Bagatelle Club, whcrc — frankly — you're not playing with amateurs and there's the peril of wasting a whole evening shuffling and betting with other sharps who a) can't be rooked so easily and b) are liable to be as cash-poor as oneself. Otherwise, it was a matter of beetling up and down Piccadilly all afternoon in the hope of spotting a ten-bob note in the gutter, or — if it came to it — dragging Farmer Giles into a side-street, splitting his head and lifting his poke. A come-down after Kali's Kitten, but needs must . . .

"It's 'Basher' Moran, in't it?" drawled someone, prompting me to look up from the gutter. "Still shooting anything that draws breath?"

"Archibald Stamford, esquire. Still practicing auntie's signature?"

I remembered Archie from some police cells in Islington. All charges dropped and apologies made, in my case. Being "mentioned in despatches" carries some weight with beaks, certainly more than the word of a tradesman in a celluloid collar you clean with india-rubber and his hideous daughter. Six months jug for the fumbling forger, though. He'd been pinched trying to make a withdrawal from a relative's bank account.

If his clothes were anything to go by, Stamford had risen in his profession. Stick-pin and cane, dove-grey morning coat, curly-brimmed topper and good boots. His whole manner, with that patronising hale-fellow-snooks-to-you tone, suggested he was in funds — which made him my long-lost friend.

The Criterion was handy nearby, so I suggested we repair to the Bar for drinks, assuming the question of who paid for them would be settled when Archie was fuddle-headed from several whiskies. I fed him that shut-out-of-my-usual-suite line, and considered a hard luck story trading on my status as hero of the Jowaki Campaign — though I doubted if an inky-fingered felon would put much stock in far-flung tales of imperial daring.

Stamford's eyes shone in a manner that reminded me unpleasantly of my late feline dancing partner. He sucked on his teeth, torn between saying something and keeping mum. It was a manner I would soon come to recognise, as common to those in the employ of my soon-to-be benefactor.

"As it happens, Bash old chap, I know a billet that might suit you. Comfortable rooms in Conduit Street, above Mrs Halifax's establishment. Do you know Mrs H?"

"Used to keep a knocking-shop in Stepney? Lazy eye and a derringer in her bustle?"

"That's the one. She's West End now. Part of a combine, you might say. A newly-established firm that's thriving."

"What she sells is always in demand."

"True, but it's not just the whoring. There's other business. A man of vision, you might say, has been doing some thinking. About my line of trade, and Mrs Halifax's, and, as it were, yours."

I was about at the end of my rope with Archie. He was talking in a familiar, insinuating, creeping-round-behind-you-with-a-cosh manner that I didn't like one bit. Implying that I was a tradesman did little for my ruddy temper. I was strongly tempted to give him one of my specialty thumps, which involves a neat little screw of my big fat regimental ring into the old eyeball, and see how his dove grey coat looked with dirty great blobs of snotty blood down the front. After that, a quick fist into his waistcoat gut would leave him gasping, and give me the chance to fetch away his watch and chain, plus any cash he had on him. Of course, I'd check the spelling of "Bank of England" on the notes before spending them. I could make it look like a difference of opinion between gentlemen. And no worries about it coming back to me. Stamford wouldn't squeal to the peelers, and if he wanted to pursue the matter I could always give him a second helping.

"I wouldn't," he said, as if he could read my mind.

That was a dash of Himalayan melt-water to the face.

Catching sight of myself in the long mirror behind the bar, I saw my cheeks had gone a nasty shade of red, more vermillion than crimson. My fists were knotted, white-knuckled, around the rail. This, I understood, was what I looked like before I "went off." You can't live through all I have without "going off" from time to time. Usually, I "came to" in handcuffs between policemen with black eyes. The other fellow or fellows or lady is too busy being carried off to hospital to press charges.

Still, a "tell" is a handicap for a card-player. And my red face gave warning.

Stamford smiled, like someone who knows there's a confederate behind the curtain with a bead drawn on the back of your neck and a finger on the trigger.

Libertè, hah!

"Have you popped your guns, Colonel?"

I would pawn, and indeed have pawned, the family silver. I'd raise money on my medals, ponce my sisters (not that anyone would pay for the hymn-singing old trouts), and sell Royal Navy torpedo plans to the Russians, but a man's guns are sacred. Mine were at the Anglo-Indian Club, nicely oiled and wrapped and packed away in cherrywood cases, along with a kit-bag full of assorted cartridges. If any big cats got out of Regent's Park Zoo, I'd be well set-up to use a Hansom for a howdah and track the vermin along Oxford Street.

Stamford knew from my look what an outrage he had suggested. This wasn't the red-hot pillar-box-faced Basher bearing down on him, this was the deadly icy calm of — and other folks have said this, so it's not just me boasting — "the best heavy game shot that our Eastern Empire has produced."

"There's a fellow," he continued, nervously, "this man of vision I mentioned. In a roundabout way, he is my employer. Probably the employer of half the folk in this room, whether they know it or not . . ."

He looked about. It was the usual shower: idlers and painted dames, jostling each other with stuck-on smiles, reaching sticky fingers into jacket-pockets and up loose skirts, finely-dressed fellows talking of "business" which was no more than powdered thievery, a scattering of moon-faced cretins who didn't know their size-thirteens gave them away as undercover detectives.

Stamford produced a card and handed it to me.

"He's looking for a shooter . . ."

The fellow could *never* say the right thing. I am a shot, not a shooter. A sportsman, not a keeper. A gun, not a gunslinger.

Still, game is game . . .

" . . . and you might find him, well, interesting."

I looked down at the card. It bore the legend PROFESSOR JAMES MORIARTY, and an address in Conduit Street.

"A professor, is it?" I sneered. I imagined a dusty coot like the stick-men who'd bedevilled me through Eton and Oxon. Or else a music-hall slickster, inflating himself with made-up titles. "What might he *profess*, Archie?"

Stamford was a touch offended, and took back the card. It was as if Archie were a new convert to Popism and I'd farted during a sermon from Cardinal John Henry Newman.

"You've been out of England a long time, Basher."

He summoned the barman, who had been eyeing us with that fakir's trick of knowing who was most likely, fine clothes or not, to do a runner.

"Will you be paying now, sirs?"

Stamford held up the card and shoved it in the man's face.

The barman went pale, dug into his own pocket to settle the tab, apologised profusely and backed off in terror.

Stamford just looked smug as he handed the card back to me.

"**Y**ou have been in Afghanistan, I perceive," said the Professor.

"How the devil did you know that?" I asked in astonishment.

His eyes caught mine. Cobra-eyes, they say. Large, clear, cold and fascinating. I've actually met cobras, and they aren't half as deadly — trust me. I imagine Moriarty left off mathematics tutoring because his pupils were too terrified to con their two-times table. I seemed to suffer his gaze for a full minute, though only a few seconds passed. It had been like that in the hug of Kali's Kitten. I would have sworn on a stack of well-thumbed copies of *The Pearl* that the mauling went on for an hour of pain, but the procedure was over inside thirty seconds. If I'd had a Webley on my hip, I might have shot the Professor in the heart on sheer instinct — though it's my guess bullets wouldn't dare to enter him. He had a queer unhealthy light about him. Not unhealthy in himself, but for everybody else.

Suddenly, pacing distractedly about the room, head wavering from side to side as if he had two dozen extra flexible bones in his neck, he began to rattle off facts, as if cramming some dullwit child for an examination.

Facts about me.

"... you are lately retired from your regiment, resigning at the request of a superior to avoid the mutual disgrace of dishonourable discharge; you have suffered a serious injury at the claws of a beast, are fully-recovered physically, but worry that your *nerve* might have gone; you are the son of a late Minister to Persia and have two sisters, your only living relatives beside a number of unacknowledged half-native illegitimates on three continents; you are addicted, most of all to gambling, but also to sexual congress, spirits, the murder of animals, and the fawning of a duped public; most of the time, you blunder through life like a bull, snatching and punching to get your own way, but in moments of extreme danger you are possessed by a strange serenity that has enabled you to survive situations which would have killed another man five times over; in fact, your true addiction is to danger, to fear — only near death do you feel alive; you are unscrupulous, amoral, habitually violent and, at present, have no means of income, though your tastes and habits require a constant inflow of money ..."

Throughout this performance, I took in Professor James Moriarty. Tall, stooped, hair thin at the temples, cheeks sunken, wearing a dusty (no, *chalky*) frock-coat, sallow as only an indoorsman can be, yellow cigarette-stain between his first and second fingers, teeth to match. And, obviously, very pleased with himself.

He reminded me of Gladstone gone wrong. With just a touch of a hill-chief who had tortured me with fire-ants.

But I had no patience with his lecture. Frankly, I'd eaten enough of that from the *pater* for a lifetime.

"Tell me something I *don't* know," I interrupted ...

The Professor was unpleasantly surprised. It was as if no one had ever dared break into one of his speeches before. He halted in his tracks, swivelled his skull and levelled those shotgun-barrel holes at me.

"I've had this done at a bazaar," I continued. "It's no great trick. The fortune-teller notices tiny little things and makes good guesses — you can tell I gamble from the marks on my cuffs, and was in Afghanistan by the colour of my tan. If you spout with enough confidence, you score so many hits the bits you get wrong — like that tommyrot about being addicted to danger — are swallowed and forgotten. I'd expected a better show from your advance notices, 'Professor'."

He slapped me across the face, swiftly, with a hand like wet leather.

Now, *I* was amazed.

I knew I was vermillion again, and my dukes went up.

Moriarty whirled, coat-tails flying, and his boot-toe struck me in the groin, belly, and chest. I found myself sat in a deep chair, too shocked to hurt, pinned down by wiry, strong hands which pressed my wrists to the armrests, with that dead face close up to mine and those eyes horribly filling the view.

That calm he mentioned came on me. And I knew I should just sit still and listen.

"Only an idiot *guesses* or *reasons* or *deduces*," the Professor said, patiently. He withdrew, which meant I could breathe again and become aware of how much pain I was in. "No one comes into these rooms unless I know *everything* about him that can be found out through the simple means of asking behind his back. The public record is easily filled in by looking in any one of a number of reference books, from the *Army Guide* to *Who's Who*. But all the interesting material comes from a man's enemies. I am not a conjurer, Colonel Moran. I am a scientist."

There was a large telescope in the room, aimed out of the window. On the walls were astronomical charts and a collection of impaled insects. A long side-table was piled with brass, copper and glass contraptions that I took for parts of instruments used in the study of the stars or navigation at sea. That shows I wasn't yet used to the Professor. Everything about him was lethal, and that included his assorted bric-a-brac.

It was hard to miss the small kitten pinned to the mantelpiece by a jack-knife. The skewering had been skilfully done, through the velvety skin-folds of the haunches. The animal mewled from time to time, not in any especial pain.

"An experiment with morphine derivatives," he explained. "Tibbles will let us know when the effect wears off."

Moriarty posed by his telescope, bony fingers gripping his lapel.

I remembered Stamford's manner, puffed up with a feeling he was protected somehow but tinged with terror that the great power to which he had sworn allegiance might capriciously or justifiably turn on him with destructive ferocity. I remembered the Criterion barman digging into his own pocket to settle our bill — which, I now realised, was as natural as the Duke of Clarence licking his own stamps or Florence Nightingale giving sixpenny knee-tremblers in D'Arblay Street.

Beside the Professor, that ant-man was genteel.

"Who *are* you?" I asked, unaccustomed to the reverential tone I heard in my own voice. "*What* are you?"

Moriarty smiled his adder's smile.

And I relaxed. I *knew*. My destiny and his wound together. It was a sensation I'd never got before upon first meeting a man. And when I'd had it from women, the upshot ranged from disappointment to attempted murder. Understand me, Professor James Moriarty was a hateful man, the most hateful, *hateable* creature I have ever known, not excluding Sir Augustus and Kali's Kitten and the Abominable Bloody Snow-Bastard and the Reverend Henry James Prince. He was something man-shaped that had crawled out from under a rock and moved into the manor house. But, at that moment, I was *his*, and I remain his forever. If I am remembered, it will only be because I knew *him*. From that day on, he was my father, my commanding officer, my heathen idol, my fortune and terror and rapture.

God, I could have done with a stiff drink.

Instead, the Professor tinkled a silly little bell and Mrs Halifax trotted in with a tray of tea. One look and I could tell she was *his,* too. Stamford had understated the case when he said half the folk in the Criterion Bar worked for Moriarty. My guess is that, at bottom, the whole world works for him. They've called him the Napoleon of Crime, but that's just putting what he is, what he *does*, in a cage. He's not a criminal, he is crime itself, sin raised to an art-form, a church with no religion but rapine, a God of Evil. Pardon my purple prose, but there it is. Moriarty brings things out in people, things from their depths.

He poured me tea.

"I have had an eye on you for some time, Colonel Moran. Some little time. Your dossier is thick, in here . . ."

He tapped his concave temple.

Later, I learned this was literally true. He kept no notes, no files, no records, no address-book or appointment-diary. It was all in his head. Someone who knows tons more than I do about sums told me that Moriarty's greatest feat was to write that book no one can make head or tail of, *The Dynamics of an Haemorrhoid* or whatever, in perfect first draft. From his mind to paper, with no preliminary notations or pencilled workings, never thinking forward to plan or skipping back to correct. As if he were singing "one long, pure note of astro-mathematics, like a castrato nightingale delivering a hundred-thousand-word telegram from Prometheus."

"You have come here, to these rooms, and you have already seen too much ever to leave . . ."

An ice-blade slid through my ribs into my heart.

". . . except as, we might say, *one of the family.*"

The ice melted, and I felt tingly and warm. With the phrase, *one of the family*, he had arched his eyebrow invitingly.

He stroked Tibbles, which was starting to leak and make nasty little noises.

"We are a large family, many cells who have no knowledge of each other, devoted to varied pursuits. Most, though not all, are concerned with money. I own that other elements of our enterprise interest me far more. We are alike in that, you will be surprised to learn. You only think you gamble for money. In fact, you gamble to lose. You even hunt to lose, knowing you must eventually be eaten by a predator more fearsome than yourself. For you, it is an emotional, instinctual, sensual thrill. For me, there are intellectual, aesthetic, spiritual rewards. But, inconveniently, money must come into it. A great deal of money."

As I said, he had me sold already. If a great deal of money was to be had, Moran was in.

"The organisation is available for contract work. You understand? We have clients, who bring problems to us. We solve them, using whatever skills we have to hand. If there is advantage to us beyond the agreed fee, we seize it. . . ."

He made a fist in the air, as if squeezing a microbe to death.

". . . if our interests should happen to run counter to those of the client, we settle the matter in such a way that we are ultimately convenienced while our patron does not realise precisely what has happened. This, also, you understand?"

"Too right, Professor," I said.

"Good. I believe we shall have satisfaction of each other."

I sipped my tea. Too milky, too pale. It always is after India. I think they put curry-powder in the pot out there, or else piddle in the sahib's crockery when he's not looking.

"Would you care for one of Mrs Halifax's biscuits?" he asked, as if he were the vicar entertaining the chairwoman of the beneficent fund. "Vile things, but you might like them."

I dunked and nibbled. Mrs H was a better madam than baker. Which led me to wonder what fancies might be buttered up in the rooms below the Professor's lair.

"So, Colonel Moran, I take pleasure in appointing you as the head of one of our most prestigious divisions. It is a post for which you are eminently qualified by achievement and aptitude. Technically, you are superior to all in this firm save myself. You are expected to take up residence here, in this building. A generous salary comes with the position. And profit participation in, ah, "special projects." One such matter is at hand, and we shall come to it when we receive our next caller, Mister — no, not Mister, *Elder* — Elder Enoch J Drebber of Cleveland, Ohio."

He consulted his watch.

"I'm flattered. And a 'generous salary' would solve certain of *my* problems, not to mention the use of a London flat. But, Moriarty, what is this *division* you wish me to head? Why am I such a perfect fit for it? What, specifically, is its business?"

Moriarty smiled again.

"Did I omit to mention that?"

"You know damn well you did!"

"Murder, my dear Moran. Its business is Murder."

Barely ten minutes after my appointment as Chief Executive Director of Homicide, Ltd., I was awaiting our first customer.

I mused humorously that I might offer an introductory special, say a garrotting thrown in *gratis* with every five poisonings. Perhaps there should be a half-rate for servants? A sliding scale of fees, depending on the number of years a prospective victim might reasonably expect to have lived had a client not retained our services?

Again, I was not yet thinking the Moriarty way. Hunting I knew to be a serious avocation. Murder was for bounders and cosh-men, hardly even killing at all. It wasn't that I was squeamish about taking human life. Quakers don't get decorated after punitive actions against Afghan tribesmen. It was simply that not one of the heap of unwashed heathens I'd laid in the dust in the service of Queen and Empire had given me a quarter the sport of the feeblest tiger I ever bagged.

Shows you how much I knew.

The Professor chose not to receive Elder Drebber in his own rooms, but made use of the brothel parlour, which was well supplied with plushly upholstered divans, laden at this early evening hour with plushly upholstered tarts. It occurred to me that my newfound position with the firm might entitle me to handle the goods. I even took the trouble mentally to pick out two or three bints who looked ripe for what ladies the world over have come to know as the Basher Moran Special. Imagine the Charge of the Light Brigade between silk sheets, or over a dresser table, or in an alcove of a Ranee's Palace, or up the Old Kent Road, or . . . well, any place really. As our pioneer padre said: When the urge surges, it must be purged.

As soon as I sat down, the whores paid attention, cooing and fluttering like doves, positioning themselves to their best advantage. As soon as the Professor walked in, the flock stood down, finding minute imperfections in fingernails or hair that needed to be rectified. Moriarty looked at the dollies and then at me, constructing something on his face that might have passed for a salacious, comradely leer but came out *wrong*. The bare-teeth grin of a chimpanzee, taken for a cheery smile by sentimental zoo visitors, is really a frustrated snarl of penned, homicidal fury. The Professor also had an alien range of expression, which others misinterpreted at their peril.

Mrs Halifax ushered in our American callers.

Enoch J Drebber — why d'you think Yankees are so keen on those blasted middle initials? — was a barrel-shaped fellow, *sans* moustache but with a fringe of tight black curls all the way round his face. He wore simple, expensive black clothes and a look of fixed stern disapproval.

The girls ignored him. I sensed he was on the point of fulminating.

I didn't need one of the Professor's "background checks" to get Drebber's measure. He was one of those odd-godly bods who get voluptuous pleasure from condemning the fleshly failings of others. As a Mormon, he could bag as many wives as he wanted — on-tap whores and unpaid skivvies coralled together. His right eye roamed around the room, on the scout for the eighth or ninth Mrs Drebber, while his left was fixed straight ahead at the Professor.

With him came a shifty cove by the name of Brother Stangerson who kept quiet but paid attention.

"Elder Drebber, I am Professor Moriarty, and this is Colonel Sebastian Moran, late of the First Bengalore . . ."

Drebber coughed, interrupting the niceties.

"You're who to see in this city if a Higher Law is called for?"

Moriarty showed empty hands.

"A man must die, and that's the story," said Drebber. "He should have died in South Utah, years ago. He's a murderer, plain and flat, and an abductor of women. Hauled out his six-gun and shot Bishop Dyer, in front of the whole town. That's a crime against God. Then fetched away Jane Withersteen, a good Mormon woman, and her adopted child, Little Fay. He threw down a mountain on his pursuers, crushing Elder Tull and many good Mormon men. Took away gold that was rightful property of the Church, stole it right out of the ground. The Danite Band have been pursuing him ever since . . ."

"The Danites are a cabal within the Church of Latter-Day Saints," explained Moriarty.

"God's good right hand is what we are," insisted Drebber. "When the laws of men fail, the unworthy must be smitten, as if by lightning."

I got the drift. The Danites were cossacks, assassins, and vigilantes wrapped up in a Bible name. Churches, like nations, all seem to need a secret police force to keep the faithful in line.

"Who is this, ah, murderer and abductor?" I asked.

"His name, if such a fiend deserves a name, is *Lassiter*. Jim Lassiter."

This was clearly supposed to get a reaction. The Professor kept his own council. I admitted I'd never heard of the fellow.

"Why, he was the fastest gun in the South-West. Around Cottonwoods, they said he struck like a serpent, drawing and discharging in one smooth, deadly motion. Men he killed were dead before they heard the sound of the shot. Lassiter could take a man's eye out at three hundred yards with a pistol."

That's a fairy story. Take it from someone who knows shooting. A side-arm is handy for close-work, as when, for example, a tiger has her talons in your tit. With anything further away than a dozen yards, you might as well *throw* the gun as fire it.

I kept my scepticism to myself. The customer is always right, even in the murder business.

"This Lassiter fellow," I ventured. "Where might he be found?"

"In this very city," Drebber decreed. "We are here, ah, on the business of the Church. The Danites have many enemies, and each of us knows them all. Oddly, I was half-expecting to come across another such pestilence, a cur named Jefferson Hope who need not concern you, but it was Lassiter I happened upon, walking in your Ly-cester Square on Sunday afternoon. It was the Withersteen woman I saw first, then the girl, chattering for hot chestnuts. I knew the apostate for who she was at once. She has been thrice condemned and outcast . . ."

"You said she was abducted," put in the Professor. "Now you imply she is with Lassiter of her own will?"

"He's a Devil of persuasion, to make a woman refuse an Elder of the Church and run off with a damned Gentile. She has no mind of her own, like all women, and cannot fully be blamed for her sins. . . ."

If Drebber had a horde of wives around the house and still believed that, he was either very privileged or very unobservant.

"Still, she must come to heel. Though the girl will do as well. A warm body must be taken back to Utah, to come into her inheritance."

"Cottonwoods," said Moriarty. "The ranch; the outlying farms; the cattle; the race-horses; and — thanks to those inconveniently-upheld claims — the fabulous gold-mines of Surprise Valley."

"The Withersteen property, indeed. When it was willed to her by her father, a great man, it was on the understanding she would become the wife of Elder Tull, and Cottonwoods would come into the Church. Were it not for this Lassiter, that would have been the situation."

It was profit, not parsons, behind this business.

"Are we to understand, Elder, that the Withersteen property will come to the girl, Fay, upon the death of the adoptive mother?"

"That is the case."

"But one or other of the females must be alive to suit the Church?"

"Indeed so."

"Which would you prefer? The woman or the girl?"

"Jane Withersteen is the more steeped in sin, so there would be a certain justice . . ."

". . . if she were topped, too," I finished his thought.

Elder Drebber wasn't comfortable with that, but nodded.

"Are these three going by their own names?"

"They are not," said Drebber, happier to condemn enemies than contemplate his own schemes against them. "This Lassiter has steeped his women in falsehood, making them bear repeated false witness, over and over. That such crimes should go unpunished is an offence to God Himself . . ."

"Yes, yes, yes," I said. "But what names are they using, and where do they live?"

Drebber was tugged out of his tirade, and thought hard. "I caught only the false name of Little Fay. The Withersteen woman called her 'Rache,' doubtless a diminutive for the godly name 'Rachel' . . ."

"Didn't you think to tail these, ah, varmints, to their lair?"

Drebber was offended. "Lassiter is the best tracker the South-West has ever birthed. And that's including Apaches. If I dogged him, he'd be on me faster'n a rattler on a coon."

The Elder's vocabulary was mixed. Most of the time, he remembered to sound like a preacher working up a lather against sin and sodomy, but slipped in was a sprinkling of terms that showed him up for — in picturesque "Wild West" terms — a back-shooting, claim-jumping, cow-rustling, water-hole-poisoning, horse-thieving, side-winding, owlhoot son-of-a-bitch.

"Surely he thinks he's safe here and will be off his guard?"

"You don't know Lassiter."

"No, and, sadly for us all, neither do you. At least, you don't know where he hangs his hat. Which I presume is one of those ten-gallon things."

Drebber was quite deflated. I enjoyed that.

"Mr and Mrs James Lassiter and their daughter Fay currently reside at The Laurels, Streatham Hill, under the names Jonathan, Helen, and Rachel Laurence."

Drebber and I looked at the Professor. He had enjoyed showing off.

Even Stangerson clapped a hand to his sweaty forehead.

"Considering that there's a fabulous gold mine at issue, I consider fifty thousand pounds sterling a fair price for contriving the death of Mr Laurence," said Moriarty, as if putting a price on a fish supper. "With an equal sum for his lady wife."

Drebber nodded again, once.

"And the girl comes with the package?"

"I think a further hundred thousand for her safekeeping, to be redeemed when we give her over into the charge of your church."

"Another hundred thousand pounds?"

"Guineas, Elder Drebber."

He thought about it, swallowed, and stuck out his paw.

"Deal, Professor . . ."

Moriarty regarded the American's hand. He turned and Mrs Halifax was beside him with a salver bearing a document.

"Such matters aren't settled with a handshake, Elder Drebber. Here is a contract, suitably circumlocutionary as to the precise nature of the services Colonel Moran will be performing, but meticulously exact in detailing payments entailed and the strict schedule upon which monies are to be transferred. It's legally binding, for what that's worth, but a contract with us is mostly enforcible under what you have referred to as a Higher Law . . ."

The Professor stood by a lectern, which bore an open, explicitly-illustrated volume of the sort often found in establishments like Mrs Halifax's for occasions when inspiration flags. He unrolled the document over a coloured plate, then plucked a pen from an inkwell and presented it to Drebber.

The Elder made a pretence of reading the rubric, and signed.

Professor Moriarty pressed a signet-ring to the paper, impressing a stylised M below Drebber's dripping scrawl.

The document was whisked away.

"Good day, Elder Drebber."

Moriarty dismissed the client, who backed out of the room.

"What are you waiting for?" I said to Stangerson, who stuck on the hat he had been fiddling with and scarpered. One of the girls giggled at his departure, then remembered herself and pretended it was a hiccough. She still paled under her rouge at the Professor's sidelong glance.

"Colonel Moran, have you given any thought to hunting a *Lassiter*?"

A jungle is a jungle, even if it's in Streatham and is made up of neat little villas named after shrubs.

In my coat-pocket I had my Webley.

If I were one of those cow-boys, I'd have notched the barrel after filling Kali's Kitten's heart with lead. Then again, even if I only counted white men and tigers, I didn't own any guns with a barrel long enough to keep score. A gentleman doesn't need to list his accomplishments or his debts, since there are always clerks to keep tally. I might not have turned out to be a pukka gent, but I was flogged and fagged at Eton beside future cabinet ministers and archbishops, and some skins you never shed.

It was bloody cold, as usual in London. Not raining, no fog — which is to say, no handy cover of darkness — but the ground chill rose through my boots and a nasty wind whipped my face like wet pampas grass.

The only people outside this afternoon were hurrying about their business with scarves around their ears, obviously part of the landscape. I had decided to toddle down there and poke around, as a preliminary to the business in hand. Call it a recce.

Before setting out on this safari, I'd had the benefit of a lecture from the Professor. He had devoted a great deal of thought to murder. He could have written the *Baedeker's* or *Bradshaw's*, though it would probably have to be published anonymously — *A Complete Guide to Murder*, by "A Distinguished Theorist" — and then be liable to seizure or suppression by the philistines of Scotland Yard.

"Of course, Moran, murder is the easiest of all crimes, if murder is all one has in mind. One simply presents one's card at the door of the intended murderee, is ushered into his sitting room and blows his or, in these enlightened times *her*, brains out with a revolver. If one has omitted to bring along a firearm, a handy poker or candlestick will serve. Physiologically, it is not difficult to kill another person, to perform outrages upon a human *corpus* which will render it a human *corpse*. Strictly speaking, this is a successful murder. Of course, then comes the second, far more challenging part of the equation, *getting away with it*."

I had been stationed across the road from the Laurels for a quarter of an hour, concealed behind bushes, awaiting signs of Lassiter. Then I noticed I was in Streatham Hill *Rise* not Streatham Hill *Road*. This was quite another Laurels, with quite another set of residents. This was a boarding house for genteel folk of a certain age. I was annoyed enough with myself and the locality to consider potting the landlady just for the practice.

If I held the deeds to this district and the Black Hole of Calcutta, I'd live in the Black Hole and rent out Streatham. Not only was it beastly cold, but stultifyingly dull. Row upon monotonous row of the Lupins, the Laburnams, the Leilandiae, and the Laurels. No wonder I was in the wrong spot.

"It is a little-known fact that most murderers don't care about *getting away with it*. They are possessed by an emotion — at first, perhaps, a mild irritation about the trivial habit of a wife, mother, master, or mistress. This develops over time, sprouting like a seed, to the point when only the death of another person will bring peace to our typical murderer. These poor souls go happy to the gallows, free at last of another's clacking false teeth or unconscious chuckle or penny-pinching. We shun such as *amateurs*. They undertake the most profound action one human being can perform upon another, and *fail to profit* from the enterprise."

No, I had not thought to purchase one of those penny-maps. Besides, anyone on the street with a map is obviously a stranger. Thus the sort who, after the fact, lodges in the mind of witnesses. "Did you see anyone suspicious in the vicinity, Madam Busy-Body?" "Why yes, Sergeant Flat-Foot, a lost-looking fellow, very red in the face, peering at street signs. Come to think of it, he *looked* like a murderer. And he was the very spit and image of that handsome devil whose picture was in the *Illustrated Press* after single-handedly seeing off the Afghan hordes that time."

"Our business is murder for profit, killing for cash," Moriarty had put it. "We do not care about our clients' motives, providing they can meet the price. They may wish murder to gain an inheritance, inflict revenge, make a political point, or from sheer spite. In this case, all four conditions are in play. The Danite Band, represented by Elder Drebber, seek to secure the gold mine, avenge the deaths of their fellow conspirators, indicate to others who might defy them that they are a dangerous power to cross, and to see dead a foeman they are not skilled enough to best by themselves."

What was the use of a fanatical secret society if it *couldn't* send a horde of expendable minions to overwhelm the family? These Danite Desperadoes plainly weren't up there with the Camorra or the Thuggee or the Dacoits when it came to playing that game. If the cabal really sought to usurp the governance of their church, which is what the Professor confided they had in mind, a greater quantity of sand would be required.

"For centuries, the art of murder has stagnated. Edged weapons, blunt instruments and bare hands that would have served for our ancient ancestors are still in use. Even poisons were perfected in classical times. Only in the last hundred and fifty years have fire-arms come to dominate the murder market-place. And for the cruder assassin, the explosive device — whether planted or flung — has made a great deal of noise, though at the expense of accuracy. Of course, guns and bombs are loud, more suited to the indiscriminate slaughter of warfare or massacre than the precision of wilful murder. That, Moran, is something we must change. If guns can be silenced, if the skills you have developed against big game can be employed in the science of man-slaying, then the field will be revolutionised."

I beetled glumly up and down Streatham Hill.

"Imagine, if you will, a Minister of State or a Colossus of Finance or a Royal Courtesan, protected at all hours by armed professionals, beyond the reach of any would-be murderer, vulnerable only to the indiscriminate anarchist with his oh-so-inaccurate bomb and willingness to be a martyr to his cause. Then think of a man with a rifle, stationed at a window or on a balcony some distance from the target, but with a *telescopic device* attached to his weapon, calmly drawing a bead and taking accurate, deadly shots. A *sniper*, Moran, as used in war, but brought to bear in a civilian circumstance, a private enterprise. While guards panic around their fallen employer, in a tizzy because they don't even know where the shots have come from, our assassin packs up his kit and strolls away untroubled, unseen and untraced. That will be the murder of the future, Moran. The *scientific* murder."

Then the Professor rattled on about air-guns, which lost me. Only little boys and pouffes would deign to touch a contraption which needs to be pumped before use and goes off with a sad *phut* rather than a healthy *bang*. Kali's Kitten would have swallowed an air-gun whole, and taken an arm along with it. The smell of cordite, that's the stuff — better than cocaine any day of the month. And the big bass drum thunder of a gun *going off*.

Finally, I located the right Laurels.

Evening was coming on. Gaslight flared behind net-curtains. More shadows to slip in. I felt comfy, as if I had thick foliage around me. My ears pricked for the pad of a big cat. I found a nice big tree and leaned against it.

I took out an instrument Moriarty had issued from his personal collection, a spy-glass tricked up to look like a hip-flask. Off came the stopper and there was an eye-piece. Up to the old ocular as if too squiffy to crook the elbow with precison, and the bottom of the bottle was another lens. Brought a scene up close, in perfect, sharp focus.

Lovely bit of kit.

I saw into the front-parlour of the Laurels. A fire was going, and the whole household was at home. A ripening girl, who wore puffs and ribbons more suited to the nursery, flounced around tiresomely. I saw her mouth flap, but — of course — couldn't hear what she was saying. A handsome woman sat by the fire, nodding and doing needlework, occasionally flashing a tight smile. I focused on the chit, Fay-called-Rachel, then on the mother, Helen Laurence-alias-Jane Withersteen. I recalled the "daughter" was adopted, and wondered what that was all about. The woman was no startler, with grey in her dark hair as if someone had cracked an egg over her head and let it run. The girl might do in a pinch. Looking again at her animated face, it hit me that she was feeble-witted — which always suggested possibilities.

The man, Jonathan Laurence-*né*-Jim Lassiter, had his back to the window. He seemed to be nodding stiffly, then I realised he was in a rocking chair. I twisted a screw, and the magnification increased. I saw the back of his neck, tanned, and the sharp cut of his hair, which was slick with pomade. I even made out the ends of his moustache, wide enough to prick out either side of the silhouette of his head.

So this was the swiftest *pistolero* West of the Pecos?

I admit that I snorted.

This American idiocy about drawing and firing, taking aim in a split-second, is pure stuff and nonsense. Anyone who wastes their time learning how to do conjuring tricks getting their gun out is likely to find great red holes in their shirt-front (or, in most cases, back) before they've executed their fanciest twirl. That's if they don't shoot their own nose off by mistake.

History has borne me out. Bill Hickock, Jesse James, and Billy the Kid were all shot dead by folk far less famous and skilled — taken from behind or while unarmed or when asleep.

Dash it all, I was going to chance it. All I had to do was take out the Webley, cross the road, creep into the front garden, stand outside the window, and blast Mr and Mrs Laurence where they sat.

The fun part would be snatching the girl.

Carpe diem, they said at Eton. Take your shot, I learned in the jungle. Nothing ruddy ventured, nothing bloody gained.

I stoppered the spy-glass and slipped it into my breast-pocket. Using it had an odd side-effect. My mouth was dry and I really could have done with a swallow of something. But I had surrendered my real flask in exchange for the trick-telescope. I wouldn't make that mistake again. Perhaps Moriarty could whip me up a hip-flask disguised as a pocket-watch. And, if time-keeping was important, a pocket-watch disguised as something I'd never really need, like a prayer-book or a tin of fruit pastilles.

The girl was demonstrating some dance now. Really, I would do the couple a favour by getting them out of this performance.

I reached into my coat-pocket and gripped my Webley. I took it out slowly and carefully — no nose-ectomy shot for Basher Moran — and cocked it with my thumb. The sound was tinier than a click you'd make with your tongue against your teeth.

Suddenly, Lassiter wasn't in view. He was out of his chair and beyond sight of the window.

I was dumbfounded.

Then the lights went out. Not only the gas, but the fire — doused by a bucket, I'd guess. The womenfolk weren't in evidence, either.

One tiny click!

A finger stuck out from a curtain and tapped the window-pane.

No, not a finger. A tube. If I'd had the glass out, I could confirm what I intuited. The bump at the end of the tube was a sight. Lassiter, the fast gun, had drawn his iron.

I had fire in my belly. I smelled the dying breath of Kali's Kitten.

I changed my estimate of the American, and of the whole business of gun-fighting. What had seemed a disappointing, drab day outing was now a worthwhile safari, a game worth the chase.

He wouldn't come out of the front door, of course. He needn't come out at all. First, he'd secure the mate and cub — a stronghold in the cellar, perhaps. Then he could get a wall behind his back and wait. To be bearded in his lair. If only I had a bottle of paraffin, or even a box of matches. Then I could fire the Laurels: they'd have to come out and Lassiter would be distracted by females in panic. No, even then, there was a back-garden. I'd have needed beaters, perhaps a second and third gun.

Moriarty had said he could put reliable men at my disposal for the job, but I'd pooh-poohed the suggestion. Natives panic and run, lesser guns get in the way. I was best off on my tod.

I would have to rethink.

Lassiter was on his guard now. He could cut and run, spirit his baggages off with him. Go to ground so we'd never find him again.

My face burned. Suddenly I was afraid, not of the gunslinger, but of the Professor. I would have to tell him of my blunder.

One bloody click, that was all it was! Damn and drat.

I knew, even on brief acquaintance, Moriarty did not merely dismiss people from the firm. He was no mere theoretician of murder.

Moran's head, stuffed, on Moriarty's wall. That would be the end of it.

I eased the cock of the Webley shut and pocketed the gun.

A cold circle pressed to the back of my neck.

"Reach, pardner," said a deep, foreign, marrow-freezing voice. "And mighty slow-like."

My bloody father always said I'd wind up with a noose around my neck. But even Sir Augustus Moran did not predict that said noose would be strung from a pretentious chandelier and attached firmly to a curtain-rail.

I was stood on a none-too-sturdy occasional table, hands tied behind my back with taut, biting twine. Only the thickness of my boot-heels kept me from throttling at once.

Here was a how-d'you-do?

The parlour of the Laurels was still unlit, the curtains drawn. Unable to look down, I was aware of the people in the room but no more.

The man, Lassiter, had raised a bump on my noggin with his pistol-butt, which throbbed angrily.

Somehow, I had an idea this was still better than an interview with a disappointed Professor Moriarty.

On the table, by my boot-toes, were my Webley, broken and unloaded, the flask-glass, my folding knife, my (empty-ish) note-case, three French post-cards, and a watch which had a sentiment from "Violet, to Algy" engraved inside.

"Okay, Algy," drawled Lassiter, "listen up . . ."

I didn't feel inclined to correct his assumption.

"We're gonna have a little talk-like. I'm gonna ask questions, and you can give answers. You understand?"

I tried to stand very still.

Lassiter kicked the table, which wobbled. Rough hemp cut into my throat.

I nodded my understanding, bringing tears to my eyes.

"Fine and dandy."

He was standing behind me. I knew the woman was in the room too, keeping quiet, probably holding the girl to keep her from fidgeting.

"You ain't no Mormon," Lassiter said.

It wasn't a question, so I didn't answer.

The table rocked again. Evidently, it *had* been a question.

"I'm not a Mormon," I said, with difficulty. "No."

"But you're with the Danite Band?"

I had to think about that.

A very loud noise sounded, and the table splintered. A slice of it sheared away, and I had to hop to keep balance on what was left.My ears rang and it was seconds before I could make out what was being said.

"Noise-some, ain't it? You'll be hearin' that fer days."

It wasn't the bang — I've heard enough bangs in my time — it was the smell, the discharged gun smell. It cleared my head.

The noose at my throat cut deep.

I had heard — in the prefects' common-room at Eton, not any of the bordellos or dives I've frequented since since those horrible school days — that being hanged, if only for a few seconds, elicits a peculiar physiological reaction in the human male. Conoisseurs reckon this a powerful erotic, on a par with the ministrations of the most expert houris. I was now, embarrassingly, in a position to confirm the sixth-form legend.

A gasp from the woman suggested the near-excruciating bulge in my fly was externally evident.

"Why, you low, disgustin' snake," said Lassiter. "In the presence of a lady, to make such a . . ."

Words failed him. I was in no position to explain that this was an unsought-for, involuntary response.

Arbuthnot, Captain of the Second Eleven, now active in a movement for the suppression of licentious music hall performance, once maintained that this throttling business was more pleasurable if the self-strangulator dressed as a ballet-girl and sucked a boiled sweet dipped in absinthe.

I could not help but wish Arbuthnot were here now to test his theory, instead of me.

"Jim, Jim, what are we to do?" said the woman. "They know where we are. I told you they'd never give up. Not after Surprise Valley."

Her voice, shrill and desperate, was sweet to me. I knew from the quality of Lassiter's silence that his wife's whining was no help to him.

I began to see the advantages of my situation.

Again, I had been through the red rage and fear of peril and come to the cold, calm, chill clearing.

"At present, Mr and Mrs Lassiter," I began, giving them their true names, "you are pursued only by foreign cranks, whose authority will never be recognised by British law. If your story were known, popular sympathy would be with you and the Danites further frustrated. The fact that Elder Drebber engaged the services of those I represent should tell you that they can take no action by themselves."

"Who *do* you represent, Algy?"

That was the question I'd never answer, not if he shot all the legs off the table and let me kick and splatter. Even if I died, Moriarty would use spiritualist mediums to lay hands on my ectoplasm and double my sufferings.

"If I step off this table, your circumstances will change," I said. "You will be murderers, low and cowardly killers of a hero of the British Empire. . . ."

Never hurts to mention the old war record.

"Under whatever names you take, you will be hunted by Scotland Yard, the most formidable police force in the world . . ."

Well, formidable in the size of the seats of their blue serge trousers . . .

"All hands will be against you."

I shut up and let them stew.

"He's right, Jim. We can't just kill him."

"He drew first," said Lassiter.

"This isn't Amber Springs."

I imagined the climate was somewhat more congenial in Amber Springs, wherever that might be. And the community's relative lack of police-men, judges, lawyers, jailers, court reporters, and engravers for the *Police Gazette*, which in other circumstances would have given it the edge over Streatham in my book, was suddenly not a point in its favour.

Even with my ringing ears, I heard the *click*.

Lassiter had cocked and aimed his gun.

He walked around the table, so he could at least shoot me to my face. It was still dark, so I couldn't get much of a look at him.

"*Jim*," protested Helen-Jane.

There was a flash of fire. For an instant, Lassiter's fiercely-moustached face lit orange.

The table was out from under me, and the noose dragged at my adam's apple.

I expected the wave of pain to come in my chest.

Instead, I fell to the floor, with the chandelier, the rope-coil and quite a bit of plaster on top of me. I was choking, but not fatally. Which, under the circumstances, was all I could ask for.

A tutu and a sweetie would *not* have made me feel more alive.

Lassiter kicked me in the side, the low dog. Then the woman held him back. That futile boot was encouraging. The fast gun was losing his rag.

Gas-light came up. Hands disentangled me from the brass fixtures and the noose, then brushed plaster out of my hair and off my face.

I looked up, blinking, at a very pink angel.

"Wuvvwy mans," said the glassy-eyed girl, "Rache want to keep um."

Though still tied — indeed, with my ankles bound as well — I was far more comfortable in the parlour of the Laurels than I had been.

I was propped up on a divan, and Rache — the former Little Fay — was playing with my hair, chattering about her new pet. She must have been fifteen or sixteen, but acted like a six- or seven-year-old. I remembered to smile as she cooed in my ears. Children can *turn* suddenly, and I had an idea this child-minded girl could be as deadly as her foster father if prodded into a tantrum.

She introduced me to her doll, Missy Surprise. This was a long-legged, home-made, one-armed rag-doll with most of her yellow wool hair chewed off. She got her name because there was a hiding place in her tummy, where Rache kept her "pweciousnesses" — which were cigar-tubes full of sweets.

The "Laurences" were still undecided about what to do with me. It's all very well being a gunslinger, but skills that serve in the Wild West — or the jungle, come to that — need to be modified in the polite society of Streatham. Or, at least, that was the case if you were a fairplay fathead like Jim Lassiter. These were truly good, putupon people. That made them weak.

Rache was kissing my ear, wetly.

"Stop that, darling," said her mother.

Rache stuck out her lower lip and narrowed her brows.

"Don't be a silly, Rache."

"Rache *not* a silly," she staid, knotting little fists. "Rache *smart*, 'oo knows it."

Jane-Helen melted, and pulled the girl away from me, hugging her.

"Not so tighty-tight," protested Rache.

Lassiter sat across the room, gun in hand, glowering.

Earlier, he had been forced to tell a deputation of concerned neighbours that Rache had dropped a lot of crockery. No one could possibly mistake gunshots for smashing plates, but they'd retreated. Blaming the girl had put her in a sulk for a moment, and inclined her even more to take my part.

This blossoming idiot was heiress to a fabulous gold mine.

I could do a great deal worse.

"We could offer him money," said Jane-Helen, as if I were not in the room.

"He won't take money," said Lassiter, glumly and — I might add — without consulting me for an opinion.

"You, sir, Algy . . ." began the woman.

"Arbuthnot," I said, "*Colonel* Algernon Arbuthnot, Fifth Northumberland Fusiliers . . ." A right rabble, that lot. All their war-wounds were in the bum, from turning and running away. "Hero of Maiwand, Jowaki and Kandahar . . ."

I'd have claimed Crécy, Waterloo and Quebec if I thought they'd swallow it.

"*Victoria Cross.*"

" 'Toria Ross," echoed Rache, delighted.

"Colonel Arbuthnot, what is your connection with the Danite Band?"

"Madam, I am a detective. Our agency has been on the

tracks of these villains for some months, with regards to their many other crimes . . ."

She looked, hopeful, at Lassiter. She wanted to believe the rot, but he knew better.

". . . when we were alerted to the presence of several of the most dangerous Danites in London, well off their usual patch as you'll agree, we made a connection to you. Of course, we knew you were here, living under an alias. We had no reason to bother you, but these comings and goings of incognito Americans — possessed of fabulous riches, but content to live in genteel anonymity — are noticed, you know. If we could find you, so could they. We've had men on you round the clock for the last two weeks . . ."

That was a mistake. Lassiter stopped listening. Anyone who could hear a cocking pistol through a window and across the road would have noticed if he were being marked.

". . . if I'm not at my post when my replacement arrives, the agency will know that something is amiss."

Jane-Helen looked hard at me. She hadn't bought it, either.

Still, in the short term, my story would be hard to *dis-*prove. I had introduced a notion that I knew would snag, and grow. The notion that I was to be relieved, that confederates would be arriving soon.

Lassiter's sensitive ears would be twitching.

Every cat padding over a garden wall or tile falling off an ill-made roof would sound like evidence of a surrounding force to our rider of the purple sage.

"Algy wants to see Rache 'utterflee dance now," announced the girl.

She fluttered dramatically about the room, trailing ribbons, inflating sleeves, and lifting skirts. One of her stockings was bagged around her ankle.

" 'Utterflee 'utterfly, meee oh myyy," she sang.

Lassiter's face was dark and heavy. I was quite pleased with myself.

I snuck a peek at the clock on the mantel and made sure I was noticed doing it.

" 'Utterfly 'utterflee, look at meee . . ."

Lassiter chewed his moustache. Jane-Helen seemed greyer. And I was almost starting to enjoy myself again.

Then the front window smashed in and something black and fizzing burst through the curtains.

I saw a burning fuse.

Lassiter got his boot on the fuse, killing the flame.

"That's not dynamite," I said, helpfully. "It's a smoke charge. They want you to run out the front door. Into the line of fire."

I didn't mention that I'd thought of something very similar.

"Jim, they're out there," said Jane.

" 'Asty mans," said Rache, peeved by the interruption.

There was a crack. More glass broke behind the curtains. A ragged hole appeared in the velvet. I'd not heard the shot. Another shattering, and the curtain whipped with the impact. And again.

"Untie me and I can help," I said.

Lassiter wasn't sure but Jane fell for it. She did my hands while Rache unpicked the knots at my ankles. I took my Webley from the floor, shaking off the flakes of plaster. Of course, it was empty. The curtain-rail, with rope still attached, fell off the wall as another silent fusillade came. Cold wind blew through the ruined window. More panes were shot out.

The neighbours would be around again soon. This was not the thing for a respectable street.

Bullets ploughed into the floor, rucking the carpet, and the opposite wall. Our sniper had an elevated position.

I waved my gun, to attract Lassiter's attention.

He dug into his pocket and brought out a handful of bullets, which he poured into my palm. I loaded and closed the revolver. I noticed Lassiter noticing how practiced I was at the procedure. But Algy Arbuthnot, V.C., was an old soldier and daring detective so that shouldn"t be too much of a surprise.

"Where is the gun-man? Top floor of the house across the street?"

Lassiter shook his head.

"Tree in the front garden?"

Lassiter nodded.

I'd been behind that tree earlier. How long ago? I didn't know if I'd been unconscious for minutes or hours. It had been twilight when Lassiter conked me, and was full dark now. I'd have sworn no one was about when I took my watching spot, but now there were armed hostiles.

"How many?"

Lassiter held up four fingers, steadily. Then another three, with a wriggle at the wrist. He *knew* there were four men — Danites? — out there, and *felt* there might be another three besides.

I've come through scrapes with worse odds. From Moriarty's background check, I knew Jim Lassiter had, too.

"This might be a moment for one of your famous rock-slides," I ventured.

Lassiter cracked a near-smile.

"Yup," he said.

As Drebber had mentioned, Lassiter was once chased up a mountain by an angry mob and had precipitated a rocky avalanche to sweep them away. His history was studded with such dime novel exploits.

Was Drebber out there? And Stangerson? And with other guns?

My nasty suspicion was that, weighing up their contract with Moriarty & Co., the Danites had decided £205,000 was a mite steep for an evening's work. They had come to us in the first place not because they were leery of doing their own murdering but because this wasn't their city and they didn"t have any idea how to track Lassiter and his women to their hole. The Professor had come straight out and announced where they were to be found, to show off how bloody clever he was. No thought as to whether Basher might get caught 'twixt the guns. My only consolation was that Moriarty undoubtedly meant what he said about Higher Law. For breaking the deal, he'd probably exterminate the Danite Band to the last man (killing their horses and dogs, too), then arrange a cholera outbreak in Salt Lake City to scythe through the Latter-Day Saints.

I, of course, would still be dead.

Lassiter and I were either side of the window, just peeking out at a sliver of night.

Another shot.

I heard a rattling-about from one of the nearby houses. A spill of light lay on the street as a front door opened angrily. In that illumination, I glimpsed a figure, in rough work-clothes but with a pointed red hood over his entire head, gathered at the neck by a drawstring, with big circles cut out for the eyes. He held a pistol, and was drawing a bead. Our shy soul froze a moment in the light and stepped back, but Lassiter had already plugged him, reddening one of his eyeholes. He collapsed like an unstrung puppet.

An irritated, bald man in a quilted dressing-gown came out of his house, urged to make further complaint about the infernal racket. He was surprised to find a masked gunman lying dead over his front gate, obscuring the "no hawkers or circulars" sign. The neighbour looked around, astonished and even more annoyed.

"What the devil . . ."

Someone shot him, and he fell over the dead. Danite.

Oops, it might have been me. I was always one to blaze away without too much forethought.

Lassiter looked disapproval at me.

A great many curtains fell from fingers in nearby houses, and the neighbours all decided to mind their own business for the duration.

The neighbour was only winged, but made a noise about it. The fellows who had accompanied him on his earlier deputation put cotton in their ears and went back to bed.

So my shot had accomplished something.

Lassiter looked out the window, searching for another target.

From where I was, I could easily shoot him in the stomach and try to hold Drebber to coughing up the agreed fee.

Evidently he could hear the wheels turning in my head.

"Algy," he drawled, gun casually aimed my way, "how'd you like to go through the winder, and draw their fire?"

"Not very much."

"What I reckoned."

Another bomb sailed through the window, without meeting any obstruction, and rolled on the carpet, pouring thick, nasty smoke. They'd let the fuse burn down before lobbing this one.

"Is there a back door?" I asked.

Lassiter looked at me, pitying.

Upwards of four men could surround a villa, easily.

Jane looked at Lassiter, like a pioneer wife who trusts her man to save the last three bullets to keep the family out of the clutches of Injuns. I always wondered why the average covered wagon bint didn't backshoot pious Pa and learn to sew blankets and pop out papooses, but I'm well-known for my shaky grasp of morality.

"This is London, England," she said. "We left all this behind. Things don't happen like this here."

A bullet struck a framed picture of Queen Victoria, which fell onto the lid of an upright piano. More bullets drove into the instrument, making horrid sounds that Rache seemed inclined to dance to until Jane held her down.

Lassiter looked at me.

We both knew *everywhere* was like this, herbaceous border in the back garden and "Goodbye, Little Yellow Bird" sheet music propped on the piano in the parlour or no. He'd have done better going to ground in the Old Jago or Seven Dials, where life was more obviously like this — those rookeries had well-traveled rat-runs and escape routes.

The smoke was getting thick and the carpet was on fire.

I saw an empty bucket lying by the grate. The water had been used earlier to douse the fire. That was my fault.

Lassiter chewed his moustache. That was his "tell," the sign that he was about to take action.

"I"m goin' out the front door," he said.

"You'll be killed for sure," pleaded Jane.

"Yup. Maybe I can take enough of 'em with me so's you and Little Fay can get away clean. You're a rich woman, Jane. Buy this man, and men like him, and keep buyin' them. Ring yourself with guns and detectives. The Danites will run dry afore the gold."

I peeked into the road again. The groaning neighbour was doubled over on the pavement, but the dead man in the hood had been dragged off. Fire was coming from at least two points. Just harrying, not trying to hit anyone.There was someone on the roof. We could tell by the creaking ceiling.

Lassiter was filling his guns. He had two Colts with fancy-dan handles. He ought to have had holsters to draw from, but he'd have to carry them both. Twelve shots. Maybe seven men. He'd certainly get hit several times, no matter how good he was. I might even be able to put a couple in his spine as he strode manfully down the path of the Laurels and claim it was a fumble-fingered accident.

He was an idiot. If it'd been me, I'd have picked up Jane and tossed her, in a froth of skirts, through the window. She was the one they wanted, heiress to the Withersteen property. At the very least, she'd be a tethered goat to draw the big game into range.

I was cold and clear and clever again. The Professor would have been proud.

"They can't afford to kill the women," I said. "That's why they didn't throw dynamite. They want someone alive to inherit, someone they can rob through Mormon marriage."

Lassiter nodded. He didn't see how that helped.

"Stop thinking of Jane and Rache as your family," I said. "Start thinking of them as *hostages*."

If he didn't take umbrage and shoot me, we might have a chance.

"**W**e're coming out," I announced. "Hold your fire."

Rache giggled. I held the baggage round the waist, gun in her ear, and stood in the doorway.

To the girl, it was a game. She had Missy Surprise hugged to her chest. Lassiter and Jane were more serious, but desperate enough to try. They had objected that the Danites would never believe their man would harm his beloved wife and daughter. I told them to stop thinking like their upright, moral, frankly tiresome selves and put themselves in the mind-skins of devious, murderous, greedy blighters. Of course they'd believe it — they'd do the same thing with their own wives or daughters. Unspoken but obvious was that I would, too.

Indeed, here I was — ready to spread a pretty little idiot's brains on the road.It'd be a shame, but I've done worse things.

I took a step out into the garden. No one killed me, so I took another step down the path.

Lassiter and Jane came after me, backwards. The Danite perched on the roof wouldn't have a shot that didn't go through the woman.

Men came out of the shadows. Five of them, in hoods, carrying guns. All their weaponry was kitted out oddly. The barrels were as long again as they ought to be, and swelled into thick, ceramic Swiss roll shapes. Silencers. I'd heard of the things, but never seen them. Cut down the accuracy, I gathered. It was wonderful that the cat couldn't hear you firing away, but less so that you'd probably miss him with all your silent shots. I'd rather use one of Moriarty's bloody air-guns than a ridiculous contraption like that.

"Parlay," I said.

The leader of the band nodded, silly hood-point flopping. The funny thing was that the hood was useless as disguise. Most masks are. You remember faces first of all, but people are a lot more than their eyes and noses — hands and legs and stomachs and the way they stand or hold a gun or light a cigar.

I was facing Elder Enoch J Drebber.

I assumed our agreement was voided. "You don't want these lovely ladies harmed," I said.

"I only need one," responded Drebber, raising his gun.

At this range, he could plug Rache in the breast and the shot would plough through her and me, killing us both.

"Rache not like mans," she said. "Rache poo on you!"

Drebber's eyes widened in his hood-holes. Rache held up Missy Surprise, and angled the rag-doll, her fingers working the hard metal inside the soft toy.

Lassiter's second gun went off and Missy Surprise's head flew apart. The Danite on Drebber's right fell dead.

"You're next," I told Drebber.

I was sure she had been aiming at him in the first place, but he wasn't to know that.

The man on the roof decided it was time to take his shot.

His finger had probably been itching all evening. I've had trouble with fools like that on safari, so keen on not coming home without having cleaned the barrel that they need to fire an elephant-gun at the regimental water-bearer just so they could say they'd killed *something*.

Lassiter was quicker than a *bhisti*, and not struggling with a ridiculously over-weighted yard-and-a-half of rifle. The overly keen rifleman tumbled dead into the flowery bower around the front door of the Laurels.

Seven, minus three. Four.

"Drop the ironmongery, Elder," I ordered.

Rache blew a loud raspberry.

Drebber was shaking. He nodded, and guns fell onto the road.

"All of them," I said.

Hands went to belts and inside pockets and boots and special compartments and a variety of hold-out single-shots or throwing knives rattled down as well.

"Now, I think you might take your dead folks, and scarper."

The four surviving Danites did as they were told. The fellow in the bower was a good sixteen-stone lump of his many wives' fat cooking and it took two to lift him.

They had a carriage down the road, and it trundled off.

Not a bad night's work, I thought. Providing it was over.

Rache was dancing around, and I thought it a good idea to relieve Missy Surprise of her .45 calibre insides. I gave the doll back, and the girl loved it none the less for not having a head.

Jane was looking at me with something like rapt gratitude. Usually a good moment to make a proposition, but I doubted my currency with Jim Lassiter stood as high as that.

"Colonel Arbuthnot, what can we ever do to repay you?"

"You can die," said a voice I recognised. "Yes, die."

I was fuming.

Moriarty didn't deign to explain, but I had caught up on it.

Of course, he knew the Danites would try to save the fee and go for the kills on their own.

Of course, he had mentioned the Laurence address deliberately, to prompt fast action.

Of course, he had followed me and watched my travails all evening long, not intervening until the danger was over.

Of course, he had found a way to profit.

He strolled up the street, head bobbing. He was dressed all in black, for the night-time. He also had a carriage parked nearby, with Chop, his silent Chinese coachman, perched up on the box. He enquired solicitously after the neighbour, who was still making a performance of being slightly shot. Somehow, the man got the notion that he had been saved by my intervention from a conspiracy of high-ranking Masons who wanted him dead over some imagined slight. It would be a risky proposition to complain officially about such well-connected villains since they *owned* the police. He bustled inside and drew his curtains, hoping to hide from inescapable doom under his coverlets.

Then Moriarty applied himself to the murders.

I was not privy to the arrangements the Professor Moriarty made with Lassiter and Jane. I had to be in the still-smoky parlour, while Rache — excited to be up long past her bed-time — banged at the gunshot piano while singing more verses of her Butterfly Song.

At the conclusion of negotiations, Moriarty was the proud owner, through hard-to-trace holding companies, of the Surprise Valley Gold Mine. A source of fabulous wealth that would flow for years to come. Amusingly, he was now a major employer in Amber Springs, Utah. Most of the toilers in his mine were Mormons of a more respectable and less bloodthirsty bent than the Danite Band.

Jim Lassiter-Jonathan Laurence, Jane Withersteen-Helen Laurence and Little Fay Larkin-Rachel Laurence were dead, burned-to-crackling in the smoking ruins of the Laurels, Streatham. It was the gas-mains, apparently. And the neighbours had some stories to tell.

What amazed me the most was that the Professor had the corpses ready. Chop and I had to wrestle them into beds before the fatal match was struck. I suspected that Moriarty had earlier had three strangers of the right ages "Burked," but he assured Jane that the substitutes were "natural causes" paupers rescued from the anatomists' tables. She believed him, and I assume that's what counts with women like her.

He had a satchel with him, full of documents: passports, birth certificates, twenty-year-old letters, used steamer tickets, bank-books, even photographs. If the Lassiter-Laurences had wanted to assume other identities, they should have come to him in the first place, when it would have cost a lot less than a gold mine. He let Mr and Mrs Ronald Lembo of Ottawa keep a private fortune of, amusingly enough, £205,000, deposited at Coutt's. It wasn't unlimited wealth, but most people should be able to live comfortably. I'd run through it inside a week.

Jane said the Professor was a wonderful man, but Lassiter knew better. He went along, but knew he'd been bushwhacked. I now think Moriarty even contrived for Drebber to come across the Laurences in the first place. For him, a fugitive in possession of a fabulous gold mine is someone who needs their exile and outlaw life turned upside-down.

Rache was afraid of the man. She wasn't stupid, just different. She would have to learn a new name, Pixie, and to address her parents as Uncle and Aunt, but they'd adopted her in the first place.

Along with the evidence of full lives lived from birth up to this minute, the Lembos found that they had been staying — in a suite at Claridge's! — in London for several days. Their traveling trunks, including entire wardrobes, were ensconced there. I had no doubt the staff would recognise them, and they'd be offered their "usual" at breakfast the next day. The family were on a long, leisurely world tour and had tickets and reservations for Paris, Venice, Constantinople, and points East. Eventually they would fetch up in Perth, Australia.

In the coach on the way back to Conduit Street, I asked about Drebber and Stangerson.

"If anyone deserves to be murdered," I said, "it's those splitters."

The Professor smiled. "And who will *pay* us for these murders?"

"Those two I'd slaughter for free."

"Bad business, giving away what we charge for. You won't find Mrs Halifax's girls bestowing favours "on the house". No, if we were to take steps against the Danites, we would only expose ourselves to risk. Besides, as you know, giving out an address is often a far more deadly instrument than a gun or a knife."

I didn't understand and said so.

"You may recall that Elder Drebber mentioned another enemy of the Danites, one Mr Jefferson Hope. Not a fugitive, in this case, but a pursuer. A man with a deadly grudge against our clients that dates back to a business in America which is too utterly tiresome to go into at this late hour."

"Drebber was half-expecting to run across Hope," I said.

"More like he was expecting Hope to run across him. This is even more likely now. I've sent an unsigned telegram to Mr Hope, who is toiling as a cab-driver in this city. It mentions a boarding house in Torquay Terrace, Camberwell, where he might find his old friends Drebber and Stangerson. I gather they will try to get a train for Liverpool soon, and a passage home, so I impressed on Hope that he should be swiftly about his business."

Moriarty chuckled.

If you read in the papers about the Lauriston Gardens murder, the Halliday's Private Hotel poisoning and death "in police custody" of the suspect cabman, you'll understand. When the Professor sets about tidying-up, the slates are wiped clean, broken up, and buried under a foundation stone.

So, at the end of it all, I was in residence in Conduit Street, part of the family. I was the Number Two in the organisation, the Man in charge of Murder, but I had a sense of how far beneath the Number One that position ranked. I had been near-hanged and shot at, but — most of all — I was kept out of the grown-ups" business. Like Rache, who had been good enough to spring the big surprise but otherwise fondly indulged or tolerated, I wasn't party to the serious haggling, just the bloke with the gun and the steady nerve.

Still, I knew how I would even things. I have begun to keep a journal. All the facts are set down, and eventually the public shall know them.

Then we'll see whose face is red. No, vermillion.   ✗

THE DEATH OF FALSTAFF

by Darrell Schweitzer

The King was in Southampton that night.

Everyone had left me but the day before: Nym who was once to be my husband, though I had little liking for him, and Bardolph, whose nose glowed like a lantern, and the boy, and even my own Pistol, who was my husband. Off they were, to France, in their country's service, for God and gold and glory, but mostly for the gold, if you take my meaning. Now the tavern was empty and silent, as all those who had made merry in it had gone away, with even my own husband saying, "Sweet Nell is such a clever one. She will take care of everything."

So they left me, even my husband, to clean up after them in more ways than one.

And with poor Sir John still lying in the bed upstairs. It was I who was to attend to that, who would send for the undertaker and clean up the remains of Sir John's life as if I were wiping a tabletop.

Trust Hostess Nell. She can look after things.

A lot more happened on that night than just myself sitting around in the dark mourning for Jack Falstaff, though I shed many a tear, and I sat by him in the dark, I did, looking at his dim shape in the dark, his nose all sharp and his fine, round face shrunken like a winter's apple. I wasn't afraid, being with a dead corpse, because it was only Sir John and I didn't fear his ghost.

"Oh, Sir John," says I, "I hope you're in your green fields now —"

And then there was a thunderous knocking at the door. I let out a cry and dropped my little candle. I groped around and found it, but couldn't relight it, so I felt my way to the door.

Still the thundering, as if to knock the whole house down.

"Anon!" I cried. "Anon!" And to Sir John I says, "If that be the Devil come for your soul, I'll just tell him the tavern is closed and send him away."

But it wasn't the Devil at the door, instead a tall, fierce-looking fellow, richly clad, and beside him a man in arms, who might have been a soldier. I couldn't quite tell in the dark, but the one had on a black coat, like velvet, and the other wore a steel cap on his head and a sword at his side.

"Hostess Quickly?"

"Aye."

"I am called Doctor Peake."

"Well whatever you're called, what is your business?"

"Does the body of Sir John Falstaff lie within this house?"

I could not deny that it did, but before I could have any whys or wherefores, this Peake and his bully-boy brushed me aside and came in. They showed me a paper, which they said was from a Higher Authority, but of course I couldn't read it.

There was something strange. I knew they came not from the watch, or from the sheriff; and the thought hits me like a thunderbolt, My God! They are from the King! But why? The King did not love Sir John in the end. He broke his heart, and of that broken heart Sir John died. So what would the King care now?

I did as they bade me. I lit my candle from the embers and led them upstairs, then fetched a lamp when it was called for, and the one in the black coat, he that called himself a doctor, he examined Sir John most closely, peering into his eyes and ears with a kind of glass, poking and touching as if a dead man were not a dead man plain to see.

"He is beyond all physick now," says I, but the doctor just growls and says, "Silence, woman," and goes on with his prodding and poking. The armed man looked at me, then at his master, but his master said nothing more, so I was allowed to stay.

I stood there, in the dark by the door, wringing my hands in silence.

At last he was done, and Doctor Peake said to his man, "It is as I had feared."

I didn't ask him what he feared, other than that Sir John Falstaff was dead, and I didn't understand why he would be afraid of that.

The other fellow nodded and hurried downstairs and out of the house. I heard him galloping off.

"And now, Hostess," said the doctor, "if you will fetch some refreshment while we wait, here's a gold noble for you."

My eyes lit up at that, you can be sure. I snatched the coin before he changed his mind and told him for that price he could have King Solomon's Feast; but he only wanted some wine and some cold mutton and cabbage, downstairs in the common room, of course, for to eat upstairs was to invite Sir John to rise up and ask for some, as he always did enjoy his victuals.

But also, for that amount of money, Doctor Peake wanted other things of me, first my swearing my silence, and then he wanted to know divers things about Sir John, his comings and goings and who he met, especially in the last days of his life.

I told what I knew, how the King had broke Sir John's heart, and how Sir John had called for sack and drank so much you'd think he'd drown in it, and how he ate enough for five huge, fat men. Yet still there was no comfort for him in it. He tried to be merry with his old friends, but he could not.

The doctor waved his hand impatiently.

"Enough of that. Did he meet with other than his usual associates? Did he take any stranger aside and speak in a whisper? Did they mention the names Cambridge, Scroop, and Grey?"

"Why Sir, if they was whispering, how would I know what names was mentioned?"

I saw rage in his face then, a flicker, like lightning far away on a summer night; but he was a hard man, and in control of himself.

"Then there were such persons? Agents? Conspirators? Speak plainly, woman! There are those who'd have your tongue out for this!"

I was all a-flustered then, and didn't know what to say, for those were names of great men, the Earl of Cambridge, Lord Scroop of Masham, and . . . I didn't know who Grey was, but he must have been great, too, to keep such company. But when do such quality as those come to an Eastcheap tavern to talk with John Falstaff?

"You said there were conspirators —"

"Oh no, Sir, if I may be so bold, Sir. You said it. I but asked if they was whispering, how I could hear what was said."

Then the doctor was angry again, for just an instant, and he let out a long sigh, like the wind escaping from a bag, and he says, "I have been told, by one who knows you passing well, that you have a better wit and a more observant eye than one might expect from . . . your kind. Here's a silver groat if you will but tell me with whom Sir John Falstaff did converse this past week or so."

I snatched the coin quick, but all I could tell him, to be truthful was, "He did go out alone, just before he took sick, and he did say it was to meet an old friend over a matter of some money. 'So you are going to pay what you owe me?' says I. Quoth he, 'What? I owe you? After such custom as I have given you? I have brought such honour to your house. You've had a prince under your roof because of me. Meaning Prince Hal, he did, and God save him who is now our lord the King. But Prince Hal then. I think there was a tear in Sir John's eye then, because his heart was broke, but he had his little joke on me and I got never a shilling. Out he went, and he came back, his face all flushed and red, like Bardolph's nose, and his speech was slurry, so Pistol my husband and the boy that was Sir John's page helped him upstairs. Soon after Sir John was sick, and sooner after dead. That is all I know, Sir, in God's honest truth."

"Then you know enough to have perhaps come to the same conclusion as have I, that Sir John Falstaff's death was not natural, but that he was murdered."

"Jesu Christ have mercy!" I put my hand to my mouth.

"There are definite signs of poison on his body. Now the matter darkens, Mistress Quickly, and your tact is required, for this is the King's business."

I let out another little cry, and for an instant you could have knocked me over with a feather, all a-swoon was I, sorrowful and afraid, for he had said this was the King's business, which is very close to the King's doing, and Oh, what a terrible thing it had to be, how it must be the very work of the Devil, that Prince Hal, who loved Falstaff, became King Henry the Fifth, who did not, and that King, to save himself the shame of his former life, found it politic to have Sir John murdered.

If that were true, I did not want to live.

But no, I could not believe it. I prayed to God and promised to repent my sins, and Sir John's, too, if it were not so.

Doctor Peake said nothing to comfort me, but only said we should wait.

"What are we waiting for?"

"For another, who has been sent for."

So we waited.

That was all there was to do. I didn't feel like idle talk, so I busied myself, tidying this and sweeping that, and I put some wood on the fire to give us light. The doctor just sat waiting too, drumming his fingers on my tabletop like the patter of rain.

Then past ten of the clock there came hoofbeats in the street outside, and thunderous knocking again.

I went to the door but the doctor got there first, and he opened the door to let in his armed man, who he'd sent away before, and another, whose face I could not see because of his hooded cloak. I think there were more men in the street outside. I heard metal clank and clink, and heavy footsteps.

The doctor closed the door swiftly.

I could see that the newcomer was a young man, tall and strong. He had a mailed sleeve, and I saw the ring he wore, even in such poor light.

Once more I crossed myself, and repented my sins, lest I die that night.

"Is it true, then?" This stranger asks the doctor.

"Sir John is murdered, My Lord," says the doctor. "There is no doubt of it."

And the other one's voice trembled a little, and he said, "But why would someone kill a harmless old clown who couldn't conspire his way out of a cup of sack?" He was speaking from his heart, and that surprised me, and I watched him careful, like.

"Begging your pardon, Lord," says I, and I curtseys. "But if you want to go up and see him —"

It was reckless of me to say anything at all, but I was crazy with fear and grief and my thoughts all a jumble; and all the other things I wanted to ask him I couldn't find the words for, not then.

The hooded man nodded to me politely, as if I were a real lady, and said, "Your pardon, Hostess Quickly."

He held out his hand, and if he had not stopped me I would have knelt down and kissed his ring, though at that instant if I knew why I dared not admit the reason, even to myself.

"Oh no," says he. "If anyone is to ask, say only that you were visited by a gentleman this night, whose name was Henry Le Roi, while the King was in Southampton, preparing for his French war."

The doctor said, "I have purchased her silence, Lord."

"Nell always knew a good bargain, though it is not in her nature to be entirely silent, as I well know," said Sir Le Roi. I didn't ask how he knew. To me he said, "Hostess, if you will lead the way."

So I lit my candle and led them upstairs, the three of them, Sir Le Roi, who still hid his face beneath his hood, and Doctor Peake, and the soldier.

We stood before the bed where Sir John lay. I bethought me that I ought to cover him up, but they'd want to see him, so I did not.

"Poisoned, My Lord," said the doctor.

"Poor old, fat, drunk, rascally fool," said Sir Le Roi. "He once said that sack would be his poison."

"But not here, Sir," I said. "He got no poison here, though he drank overmuch, and did not always pay for it."

"That was in his nature," said Sir Le Roi.

"It would seem he was poisoned elsewhere," said the doctor, "and returned here to die."

"We must discover the murderer then," said Sir Le Roi,

"and within but a few hours, too, for I have pressing business, as you well know. Damn! But for more time!"

"We can hardly search the whole city in a few hours, Lord. Even if we knew what the criminal looked like."

"We must make him come to us. But how to get word to him? He could be anywhere."

"Likely in his bed at this hour," said the doctor.

"I think not," said Le Roi. "I think not. But let me think further. Let us plan our stratagem . . ." He began pacing back and forth, clinking and clattering beneath his cloak. "If this rogue wants Sir John dead, and thinks he is dead, then he'll feel a sense of relief that the task is completed and the tongue he wanted silenced is silenced, and this murderer, being a low fellow, will celebrate his exploit in a low manner. I think he will be in a tavern, with his comrades, saluting the completion of their enterprise. He'll be drinking a toast, which I swear will slake his thirst all the way to the gallows."

"That still does not find him, Lord."

Le Roi stopped suddenly. He struck his hand with his other fist. His ring flashed in the candlelight. "I have it! Imagine the fright the fellow would have if he were to learn that Sir John Falstaff is not dead!"

"But Sir," I broke in, amazed, "why there he is, cold and dead as you see. You cannot bring him back!"

Sir Le Roi said softly, "In Arthur's bosom, so I hear —"

"Sir!" I said, much alarmed, wondering if this Le Roi might be the very Devil, who could read my thoughts.

He turned to the doctor, to the soldier, then back to me, as if to include all of us in his council. "Hark you then. Pray to God this works."

To the soldier he said, "Station the men all about the street, out of sight, so our quarry may enter the house but not leave it."

"It shall be done, Lord," said the soldier, and off he went.

To the doctor, he said, "We must conceal ourselves. Where?" He looked about the room. There was a trunk, but barely big enough to hide a boy in it.

He turned to me.

"Mistress Quickly, is there a curtain?"

"What, Sir?"

"A drapery. A hanging of some sort."

Befuddled, I could only say, "There's just the sheets."

"It will have to do. Take you a sheet then, and hang it up on the wall like a curtain, as if to cover a window, for all theres no window there. In the dark, he'll never notice."

"Never notice what, Sir?"

"But do as I instruct you."

I did. The doctor was the taller and helped. I stood on a stool by him, and we two nailed a sheet up at the ceiling, so it hung down behind the bed, like a curtain.

Then Le Roi and the doctor hid behind the sheet.

Now this made no sense at all, and they looked like a couple of lunatics, hiding in the room from a dead man, as if this would conjure up who murdered him. I might have laughed, were I not so afraid. But if these were lunatics they might murder me and wrap me up in that sheet, and it was no laughing matter.

Sir Le Roi came out from behind the sheet and directed me downstairs, into the common room. The doctor remained where he was, hidden.

"Mistress," says he, in a low, secret voice, "would you undertake an adventure tonight — for gold?"

"I might," says I, not knowing what he meant.

"Would you do it for love of Jack Falstaff?"

"I would, for I did love him, for he was a most merry gentleman and a true friend —"

"So did we all love him," says Sir Le Roi beneath his hood. Very much I wanted to push that hood back and see his face, but I dared not.

"We?"

"All who loved him, for who did not love him?"

I couldn't contain myself any longer. Call me a fool, but I broke down into tears and cried like a baby, and I spoke my mind clearly, not caring of the result. "No, Sir, not all. First there was the murderer, who did not love him at all. But also there was the King, and God strike me dead for saying so. Prince Hal, who seemed to love Jack, did not and proved false to him when he became King, and he broke Jack Falstaff's heart when he turned him away and said he knew him not. And, Sir, it may even be that the King so wanted to quit Jack's company that he made Jack do the quitting —"

"What do you mean?" says he, and his voice was very grim, but my fire was up, and I spoke on.

"I mean that maybe it was the King that caused Sir John to quit this Earth."

There I had said it, and strike me dead.

But it was Sir Le Roi who staggered back as if struck, and he let out a little cry of, "Oh," and then "Oh no," and his voice was trembling and I think he wept. I think I could see just a glint of a tear, by the light of the fire.

He took me by both my shoulders and peered into my eyes out of the darkness of his hood, and said, "Mistress, how could you make so monstrous an accusation? It is treason, you know."

"If I hang for it, I hang for it," says I.

"Upon my honour as a Christian, you shall not hang," says he. His voice stumbled, but then gained strength. "The King is in Southampton tonight, as you well know —"

"I know it, Lord. Getting ready for the wars. My husband Pistol is with him."

"May he prove a good soldier."

I doubted he would, but didn't say so.

"What I mean to say, my dear lady," said Le Roi, "and may I be damned to Hell if I lie, is that I am a close companion of the King, and I know his mind, and I swear to you that the King still loved Jack Falstaff, for all that he, in his office as king, could not keep such company. But he provided him with a purse to buy him drink and keep a roof over his head, and, most assuredly, the King wished the old man no harm." Now he let go of me and began to saw the air with his hands, and pace about, like a hound on a leash, straining to run. Once his hood fell down, but I turned away, and he put it up quick. "What the King desires, more than anything in this world, is that Falstaff be avenged. Therefore Mistress Quickly, justify your name, and go quickly to all the other taverns in the neighborhood — and I have the King's word for it that there are many — and proclaim to all that Jack Falstaff is alive and has begun to recover his senses, and speaks in his feverishness certain names. God willing, this will frighten the murderer into coming here to finish his work, and we'll have him!"

I gaped in amazement.

"Will you do this, for sweet Jack Falstaff's sake?"

"Oh yes, Lord! I will!"

And I went out, fast as I could, to every other tavern that was open that night. I told it to people in the street, too, to anyone and everyone. "Its a miracle!" I shouted. "Jack Falstaff is alive!"

Oh, they laughed at me. They asked if Jack had changed his name to Lazarus. Somebody threw beer in my face and said I hadn't drunk enough yet. But I told the story, all excited and breathless like, of how Jack Falstaff had begun to recover from his illness — I didn't say from his poison, for that would have given the game away — and now he was back from Arthur's bosom after all and asking after some rogue who meant him harm.

"What rogue?" says they.

"Its just the fever. He's talking nonsense," says I, "but praise God, he is alive!"

When I was alone again, I cried bitter tears, wishing it were so, though I knew it was not.

And past midnight, when I'd cried and proclaimed my throat sore, and thought to drink a little sack myself for the soothing of it, I returned to my own house.

It was dark when I went in, Sir Le Roi was waiting at the foot of the stairs.

"Is it widely proclaimed?" says he.

"Aye."

"And well done," says he, and he went upstairs to hide behind the curtain.

I soothed my throat, and soothed it a bit more. I sat in the common room, soothing it, and perhaps I slept some, and dreamed of Sir John Falstaff and Prince Hal and the Devil all sitting around that table making merry, like in the old times.

Then there was a light and stealthy rapping at the door.

I took up my candle.

"Who is it?"

"A friend of Falstaff's. He wants to see me. Urgent."

I opened the door a crack. There was a big, ragged man outside, with an evil look to him, no friend of Sir John's that I ever knew.

"Is it true that Falstaff's upstairs and he's recovered?"

"It is, but he is weak and old, and cannot have visitors disturb his rest, so if you will just come back in the morning —"

I had to make myself convincing, for if I'd said, " Sure, come right up and see him," when I was supposed to be harbouring a sick man who'd almost died, the rogue would have smelled a rat, or the rat a rogue, or whichever.

Instead he shoved his shoulder against the door and came crashing in. Quick as a snake he caught me by the hair, gave a good yank, and had a dagger pointed at my throat.

"I think Sir John will see me now," says he.

"You're not his friend," says I.

"Maybe I lied. But he will see me. Lead on."

I didn't have to pretend to be afraid, because he could have butchered me like a sheep right there and found his way upstairs by himself, but I led on, and up we went, and he stood by Jack's bedside for just a moment and said, "Sir John Falstaff, Roger the Bear has come to settle an old score," and he plunges his dagger into poor Falstaff's dead heart.

Then I screamed and Sir Le Roi and Doctor Peake jumped

out from behind the hanging sheet and there was some scuffling in the dark. Doctor Peake went to the window, threw open the shutters and shouted, but by then Le Roi had wrestled Roger the Bear to the floor and it was all over.

Le Roi's hood came off then and I saw his face clear in the moonlight, the shutters being open. Our eyes met. He seemed to be saying, without any words, The King still loved Falstaff. And I knew that it was true.

But I am sworn to say that the King was in Southampton that night, preparing for the war.

And that is all there is to tell, though I do not even know the ending, really, because the house was suddenly filled with armoured men and they hauled Roger the Bear away all trussed up like they was hunters that had caught a bear, indeed.

I heard someone say, "This is no conspiracy, but some trifling matter of an old insult."

And Sir Le Roi, Henry Le Roi, him that knew the King's mind so well, though the King was in Southampton, said, "My conscience is clear."

I can only tell you what I overheard, that Roger the Bear got his name from his sheer ugliness, though I suppose he was like a wild, murdering beast. He was but a common cut-purse and cut-throat, the low, evil sort of fellow Sir John sometimes kept company with, when it was his humour, and the more his grief it was.

I can tell you that it's the way of things, histories and the doings of kings sometimes all turn on little happenings, or nothing. We is but on this world for a little time, and the leaving of it can be just a chance, like somebody stumbles and hits his head, or there's an old grudge and Sir John dumped a cup of sack over Roger the Bear when he tried to collect some money Sir John owed. Sometimes the great is small and the small is great, all mixed up, and it doesn't mean anything at all.

Sure, no comet blazed for the passing of Falstaff.

The King was in Southampton that night, as all the world knows.

But I can tell you this, too: that as they dragged Roger the Bear down the stairs and out of my tavern, the armour Henry Le Roi wore beneath his cloak rattled like the thunder of a gathering storm, and just a little while later, that storm broke upon France. ✗

TOUGH GUYS DON'T PAY
by Stan Trybulski

The old man waited silently for his visitors in the small room at the back of the night club. He sat in the shadows, a drink in his ancient gnarled hand, the mottled skin chilled by the ice in the glass. There was a floor lamp in the room but the old man kept it turned off and facing the door. He liked the darkness; he had operated in it for fifty years, wearing its shadows like a pair of old gloves.

There was a gentle rapping on the outside of the door and then it opened and Calvi, his right-hand man, entered with the young kid right behind him.

He could see the kid had on sunglasses, smoky black orbs just below a head of coiffed hair that was streaked with some kind of fancy salon product.

The kid was wearing a supple leather sports jacket over a gray silk shirt, tight trousers and a pair of expensive European shoes. The old man approved. He had been the kid's age once, had done his first kill back then, with nothing more than an ice pick. Quick and silent, up close and personal. That had become his modus operandi, and over many years it had brought him to the top of the organization's chart.

"Take off the shades," the old man growled, flicking on the floor lamp and swiveling it until it was shining directly in the other's face.

The kid hesitated but did as he was told and held his hand up to his face to block the glare of the lamp.

"Take your hand down," the old man said.

The kid lowered his hand and squinted towards the desk.

The old man had told Calvi to wait outside; he was comfortable being alone with the kid. Calvi had frisked the kid before he let him enter the room and the kid was clean. So he wasn't worried. Besides, death was a good friend to the old man. There had been many more kills after the first, and not just with an ice pick. He had used a knife, a pistol, a shotgun, acid, even electrocution. But the ice pick had been the first, and it remained the old man's favorite. He still kept one in his desk drawer, a reminder of the long, hard, bloody climb to the top. It was a fancy, custom-made job with a gold-plated handle, and he kept it in a small, velvet-lined, teak case. He never planned on using it, but why take chances? He kept the drawer open and let his left hand rest casually near the teak case.

"Tell me about the job," he said to the kid. A sharp pain ran through the old man's skull, annoying him, and he rubbed his temples, trying to make it disappear.

"I already explained everything to Calvi," the kid said.

"I run the organization, not Calvi, so explain it to me. I'm not going to tell you again."

The old man listened while the kid ran down his entire spiel about the midtown jewelry store and how easy it would be to knock it off. He let the kid finish and then said, "You know fifty per cent belongs to me, the rest you divide between your crew."

"Yes, sir," the young kid said.

"Whaddya think?" the old man asked Calvi after the kid left.

The tall, bald man shrugged.

The old man nodded. "Right, we won't need him after the job is done." He rubbed his temples again, wishing the pain would go away. He finished his drink and poured another. "Any of our girls outside?" he asked Calvi.

"Connie's at the bar."

"Send her in and close the door. I need some relaxation."

"I have some bad news," the doctor told the old man. "You have a brain tumor. Here, look at the scan."

The old man waved the wide sheet of film away. "So I got a tumor. Operate."

The doctor shook his head. "I'm afraid it's nearly impossible. The tumor is a high-grade malignant glioma, what we call a glioblastoma, and the standard treatment is an operation called a craniotomy."

"So why can't we do it?" the old man asked.

The doctor took a deep breath. "It has progressed to the point that it looks like a fried egg. I'm afraid it has tentacles that are spreading into nearby brain tissue, and complete surgical removal is almost impossible."

"What about radiation or chemotherapy?" the old man asked.

"It's too late for that," the doctor said.

"So what will happen to me?" the old man said.

"First you'll lose your vision, then control of your facial muscles, you'll have twisted expressions and drool, then your hearing will go, you'll no longer be able to swallow or speak or turn your head."

"Then what, doc?"

"Then you die."

"I don't die," the old man snarled, "I make other people die."

The doctor recoiled in fear and said nothing.

The old man glared at him. "You said surgical removal is almost impossible, right?"

"I'm afraid so."

"So it can be possible."

"The tumor is very advanced. If the operation fails, you'll be either be dead or a vegetable."

"And if we don't operate?"

"You'll be dead in weeks."

"So it has to be an operation," the old man said.

The doctor rubbed his face and chose his words very carefully. He knew who his patient was and his powerful status in the underworld. "There is only one neurosurgeon who might be able to perform the operation with some chance of success."

"Who?" the old man growled. "I'll pay whatever it takes, but get him here now."

"Her," the doctor said. "Dr. Wachsel is a woman."

The old man waved his hand. "I don't care, just get her here."

The doctor sighed. "Whatever you say. She lives in Beverly Hills but I'll reach out, send her your file and the scans. I don't know if she's available but I'll have her call you."

"Available? Tell her I'll pay whatever she wants, that should make her available."

The young nurse wheeled the old man into the prep room. It was cold and the flimsy hospital gown and thin cotton blanket did nothing to keep the chill from his shriveled body. He tried to keep his arms and shoulders away from the stainless steel frame of the gurney, each touch of the metal causing him to shiver.

The nurse noticed the goose bumps forming on the old man's spotted flesh. "It's nothing to be afraid of, sir. Dr. Wachsel is the best in the business."

The old man's lips twisted in anger. "I'm afraid of nothing, bitch," he sneered.

The nurse shook her head sadly and walked away.

The old man closed his eyes and breathed deeply. Why in the hell is it so cold in here? he groused. Where in the hell is the lady doc? They had spoken by phone four weeks ago and she had reviewed the scans that were sent her and was convinced she could operate successfully. Today was the earliest she could perform the operation and the old man hadn't argued. When she said it would be a million dollars, the old man didn't even blink. His contacts on the Coast had told him all about Wachsel and her expensive tastes, especially custommade jewelry. And after today, he'd have plenty of that. The old man had convinced her to take the million in loot, the IRS would never know, and she had gone for the deal without hesitation. The old man smiled at the thought. After this was all over, he'd send his boys out to the Coast and take the jewelry back. No sweat. Who was she going to report the robbery to? Did she really think he was going to pay? He was a tough guy, and tough guys don't pay.

Besides, he had taped the conversation and put it with the other tapes he kept, in case he ever got jammed up with the feds. At his age, the old man wasn't going to spend a day behind bars, so he had started keeping insurance. He had plenty of dough stashed away and could live real sweet in a witness protection program, if it ever came to that. The more he thought about this, the more he liked it. He would recommend his associates to her for operations on a cash basis and have her kick back a portion. Hell, she'd be the family surgeon. If she balked, he'd play the tapes. And if that didn't convince her, he'd send Calvi out for a little talk. Yeah, she'd turn out to be a nice money-maker for him.

He rubbed his arms and thought about the heist. If the kid was all he said he was, he'd be loading the satchel with a couple of mil in jewelry right about now. Then he'd be heading to the meet with Calvi. The kid said he wants to do more jobs, probably could. It's a damn shame Calvi has to waste him. But when the haul is this big, you leave no witnesses. The kid shoulda known that, the old man sneered to himself. Strictly amateur, no matter how good he thinks he is. Besides, why let the kid have half the take? Tough guys don't pay.

The mild sedative the nurse had given him was starting to kick in now and he pulled the thin prep room blanket up around his neck. Jeez, it's so freaking cold. Maybe there'll be some really good stuff in the satchel. When I'm better, he thought, I'll give Connie a present, tell her to bring her younger sister and we'll celebrate. Make the bimbos do each other, he smirked.

The old man knew the power of money. It was almost as good as a gun.

Almost.

The silver Lexus pulled into the midtown parking garage and the driver got out and opened the rear door.

"Will you be long, madam?"

A tall blonde with fine expressive hands stepped out, shaking her head. "No, have the car ready to leave in a few minutes; I'm running late."

As the tall blonde walked into the jewelry store, a dark blue Crown Vic pulled up to the curb between two NO PARKING signs. The young kid in the front passenger seat checked the nine-millimeter he was carrying and then slid it into the Velcro holster underneath his silk Armani sports coat. He put on the pair of smoky sunglasses, their dark frames matching the color of the thin leather gloves he and his partners were wearing.

The young kid had selected the two best from his crew: Perez, a young vet who spent the last fifteen months driving Humvees through the Iraqi desert, as the wheel-man, and Malloy, a baby-faced redhead very comfortable using a pistol and whose goal in life was to do a robbery for every freckle on his cheeks, as the backup.

He had thought the whole thing through before he had decided to go to the old man and get his permission to do the heist. So what if he had to kick half the take upstairs? It was worth it. When this job was over, his crew would have respect from the world; they'd be with someone full-time, with real protection. No more existing on chump change between jobs; they'd be doing loan-sharking, bookmaking, even running legit businesses. Hell, he already owned one bar, which his crew used as their office. He smiled to himself. Jewelry heists would just be gravy on the steak.

"Remember what I said," he told Perez. "As soon as we're in the back seat, peel out of here and don't stop until we reach my Viper, turn on the lights and siren if you have to. Then take the Crown Vic to Flatlands and torch it. We'll meet up at the bar."

Perez nodded, saying nothing. That's why the young kid liked him, Perez never said anything.

"I don't see why we can't come along," Malloy said.

"We have to do this the old man's way," the young kid said. "He didn't get where he is by doing things the way other people want."

"That's what worries me," Malloy said.

The young kid ignored the remark. "Let's go," he said, handing Malloy a large leather satchel.

The young kid and Malloy entered the store and calmly looked around, knowing there would be few customers at that time of day. There was only one jeweler in the establishment and they waited patiently while he was showing a tall blonde woman some very fancy pieces. The young kid noticed that the woman was holding a diamond necklace that had a large sapphire dangling from it. He would make sure to grab that first.

They browsed at the jewelry in the display cases, peering first into a corner case filled with men's rings and then at the section containing wrist watches. The young man appeared to appreciate a solid-gold Tissot watch that had a small diamond set at each hour marking. But all the while, he was keeping an eye on the tall blonde and the jeweler.

When the woman started posing with the diamond necklace in front of a mirror, the jeweler looked over at the young man and Malloy.

"May I be of help?" he said.

The young kid smiled and said, "I'd like inquire about the Tissot."

As the jeweler started to walk towards the watch display case the young man leaped over the counter and stuck his automatic under the man's jaw.

"Don't even think about pressing an alarm button," he said, prodding the underside of the man's chin.

The tall blonde turned towards them, drawn suddenly by the commotion.

"Hand me the satchel," the young kid told Malloy, who tossed it to him. Nodding at the tall blonde, he added, "Get that necklace."

"You're not going to give us any trouble, are you?" he said, jabbing the jeweler with his pistol.

The man shook his head *no*.

"Good," the young man said, opening the satchel. "Load this up, starting with the diamond rings, then the bigger pieces." He poked the man in the side with the pistol. "Hurry up."

While the young kid kept an eye on the jeweler, Malloy walked over to the tall blonde and reached for the diamond necklace. She pulled her hand back and he grabbed at it again.

"No," she said, "I'm buying this, it's mine."

"The hell you are," Malloy said, slapping the side of her head with the gun barrel.

"Now give it up."

The woman winced in pain and held her head with one hand but squeezed the diamond necklace tight in the other.

"Faster," the young kid said to the jeweler who was scooping watches into the satchel. "Get the damn necklace," he said to Malloy, who was pulling on the woman's hand.

Stepping backwards, the tall blonde tried to kick Malloy in the groin. He twisted sideways, catching the blow on his thigh, but lost his balance and started to slip. As he fell, he grabbed at the blonde with his gun hand and a round suddenly went off.

The woman slumped to the floor, blood pouring out of her upper chest.

"Damn it," the young kid shouted, firing two rounds into the jeweler's head. "Let's get the hell out of here."

The young kid pulled his Viper into an empty spot underneath the Verrazano Narrows Bridge. It was dark now and he could see the far off lights of lower Manhattan twinkling brightly in the distance. He hit the power button on the window and let some of the air from the harbor wash his face. What the hell had gone wrong? He tried to visualize the jewelry store. First Malloy shoots the woman, and then he shoots the jeweler. Two dead. Then they ran out with the satchel only half full. He rubbed his eyes. Maybe it was all for the best. The jeweler had seen their faces, so he couldn't let him live. And it was still a good haul, even if he had to turn over half to the old man. So what the hell.

The sound of gravel crunching under tires turned his attention back to the present. He looked out the window and saw a green BMW Series 7 parking next to him. Even in the gloom, he recognized Calvi's shaved head behind the wheel. He grabbed the satchel and started to get out of the Viper.

"Stay there," Calvi said, opening the door of his BMW and walking over to the young kid's car and getting into the front passenger seat. "Is that it?" Calvi asked, pointing at the satchel on the young kid's lap.

"Yeah, but we couldn't get all that we expected."

"Open it anyway," Calvi said. "Let's take a gander."

The young kid did as he was told and Calvi put his hands inside and grabbed a few pieces of jewelry and looked at them.

"Tell the old man I'm sorry that the take wasn't as large as we anticipated but a problem cropped up," the young kid said.

Calvi dropped the jewelry back into the bag. "Don't worry about it," he said, "The old man wants you to have this."

The young kid was closing up the satchel as Calvi was speaking and never saw the pistol as Calvi raised it to the side of his head and pulled the trigger. He never even heard the sound of the gunshot that sprayed bits of his skull and brain matter against the car window.

Calvi unclasped the satchel from the pair of dead hands and got out and closed the door. The old man is going to like the contents, he just knew it.

And one less amateur to screw things up. The old man will like that even better.

The old man opened his eyes when the surgical nurse entered the prep room.

"How much longer I gotta wait?" he demanded. "I'm paying you assholes a lot of dough to take care of me."

"There has been a complication, I'm afraid."

The old man stared at the nurse, fury flooding his face. "Whaddya mean complications? I pay so things aren't complicated."

The nurse kept her face expressionless.

"One of the doctors will be in shortly to explain," she said, walking to the door.

"Get him in here right now," the old man started to yell, his words trailing off to a murmur as the pain flooded into his head.

"I'm afraid there's not going to be an operation," the doctor said.

The old man looked at him through narrowed eyes. "Where's Doctor Wachsel? I want to see her, speak to her right now."

"That will be impossible," the doctor said. "There's been a serious accident."

"Accident? What accident?" The old man tried to sit up in the gurney, but sharp pains stabbed through his head and he felt sick. The nurse eased him back down onto the gurney.

"Take it slow," the doctor said. "You're a tough guy, but even you have your limits."

The old man shrugged the nurse off and tried to sit up again. "Answer me. What accident?" His face was red with rage.

The doctor looked sadly at him. "Dr. Wachsel was shot in a jewelry-store holdup. Only a few minutes ago. The police just called."

The old man's face drained of color. "Is she dead?"

"No, but she was wounded in the shoulder and won't be able to perform any surgeries for months."

"What does that mean for me?" the old man asked.

The doctor's face turned even sadder. "I'm afraid you'll be dead in forty-eight hours."

The old man fell back onto the gurney and closed his eyes.

"I really am terribly sorry," the doctor repeated. "You're a tough old bird." He turned to leave the prep room but stopped and said to the nurse, "Please call billing and tell them that the operation's cancelled and the patient doesn't pay for to-day's surgical preparation."

"I've authored over a dozen monographs on handwriting analysys, yet I can't make out a word of this prescription for foot powder you've just written for me."

VACATION FROM CRIME
by Hal Charles

Father still knew best, Kelly Locke admitted. The drive up to the fishing cabin with him had indeed helped lessen the stress. The bushes teeming with ripe blackberries and the mountain air so much cooler than the city in August supported her father's argument that they both needed a vacation — he from being Chief of Detectives in a city with one of the nation's highest crime rates and she from reporting it as *NewsTeam 4*'s chief anchor.

Since her childhood, the two of them had journeyed to the lake every summer. After her mother's death, she had accompanied her father, the local scoutmaster, up here to his summer camps. Then, a few years ago they had liked Lake Jewell so much they co-purchased the Walkers' summer place from the heirs and continued their yearly pilgrimages as a way of reaffirming their sense of family.

Stuffing her Katie-Couric-length auburn hair under her baseball cap as she exited the Trailblazer in front of the cabin, she had to laugh.

"I told you a trip up here would make you happy," commented Matt Locke.

"I was just remembering those scouts we passed at the foot of the hill. The way they were lined up at the camp entrance beside their scoutmaster with three kneeling, three standing, and three kneeling made me remember all those summers up here with you and your troops."

"Back when a girl was one of the boys." Her father chuckled in nostalgia.

"With all their colorful neckties and merit badges, you used to call my scouts The Speckled Band."

"Dad," she said, grabbing her favorite fly rod, "to be honest, I think that name was more because with all those 'For Boys Only' activities, I got stuck reading those Sherlock Holmes stories you bought me to keep my mind off being excluded."

"You could have joined the girl scouts," returned Matt Locke, starting to unpack.

"And missed all those stories of The Great Detective? Come on, Dad, we have time before dark to wet a line and see who catches that speckled band around the lake's largest trout."

"The game," said her father, "or in this case, the fish, are afoot."

Casting on the dock in day's fading light, they saw a familiar Jeep pull up to the cabin. An angular man climbed out and ambled down toward them.

"Grab your pole, Sheriff Wray," Kelly called. "The lake's stocked with enough for all of us."

"Matt, Kelly," said the newcomer, "it's great to see you two again, and I wish this was a social visit."

"There goes the vacation," joked her father.

The sheriff began buttoning his brown jacket as the cool breeze off the lake struck him. "I hate to tell you this, but there's an escaped convict around here, and folks are re-feeling that old fear."

"Sounds like the opening of one of those ghost stories you used to tell around the campfire when I was a kid," said the news anchor.

"Sorry, Miss Kelly, but Villiers is real."

Suddenly a mountain lion's early-evening snarl echoed across the calm face of the lake.

"Not Reggie Villiers?" said the Chief of Detectives.

"'Fraid so, Matt. Bludgeoned a guard at the state pen earlier this week. Got word last night he'd been spotted in Fairpoint."

"That's not ten miles from here," said Kelly, twirling a wisp of her hair, as she always did when she grew nervous.

Sheriff Wray steadied himself against one of the dock's poles and stared across the misty water. "Matt, you know why he's headed this way. He's after me. Gonna do what he promised at the courthouse."

"Come on, Porter," said the Chief of Detectives. "How many men you caught who don't promise to get you back?"

"But you never met Villiers, never looked into his dead eyes," said the sheriff. "He's not your ordinary breed of criminal. He's a lot like that lion out there, a real killer."

As long as Kelly had known him, Sheriff Wray was her friend — the tall, strong fishing buddy and storyteller who helped fill a little tomboy's summers with adventure. He had been her protector when her father wasn't around, but now, standing there and steadying himself with the pole, he suddenly looked old and strangely haggard. "What will you do, Sheriff?" she asked.

"What can I do but wait? State Police have promised to have tracker dogs here tomorrow." The lawman released his grip on the pole. "Well, it's getting late. Got to go by Camp Cochipimingo, check on the scouts like I done for twenty years, and maybe tell them a story 'bout real ghosts."

"So you're still doing that, Porter," said Matt Locke. "Way back when I was a scoutmaster, you always managed to find time to drop by the campfire."

"Everybody knows it," said the lawman, and they've come to expect it."

The two-way radio on the sheriff's shoulder crackled. "Sheriff Wray, come in. Sheriff Wray."

The lawman punched his mike. "What'a ya got, D. W.?"

"Disturbance out at Rhodes farm. Something's got Byno's cattle spooked. What's your twenty?"

"Less than five miles from there. I'm on my way. Ten-four."

Seeing his friend's body tense up, Matt Locke volunteered to go with him.

"Thanks, but those cows, and even old Byno, I can handle. You can do something for me though. Kelly, if you still remember some of those old ghost stories, I'd 'preciate it if in a couple of hours when it's good and dark you'd wander down to the campsite. There's only a small troop there this weekend."

"Be happy to," she answered, remembering the path that ran from the cabin to the nearby camping area.

"Tell 'em the one about The Hook," said the departing lawman. "That always used to scare kids, especially red-haired little girls."

Standing beside the farmer's sink, Kelly watched her father repeatedly scour the frypan that an hour earlier had cooked the first small-mouth bass of the summer. He seemed to be grinding a hole through the bottom. "Trying to wash away the past, Dad?"

"Can't be done." He washed the soap from the pan. "You were pretty quiet during supper. Thinking about The Hook?"

She knelt beside the hearth and began to lay a fire. "I'd bet we were both thinking the same thing."

"This cabin is the very place where Reggie Villiers killed his best friend, Frank Walker."

"And if he hadn't, we wouldn't have been able to buy it from his daughters." Kelly crisscrossed the crumpled newspaper with dry kindling, placing the larger sticks on the bottom as she'd been taught years ago. "You don't feel guilty, do you?"

"No, and I don't feel afraid, either," revealed Matt Locke. "But I do worry about Porter. Villiers was a strong man who would have choked Porter to death that day if the sheriff hadn't shot him in the foot."

"Those tracker dogs will find him tomorrow."

"If it doesn't rain tonight and wash away the scent."

"You really think Villiers is coming this way?" Kelly asked.

"According to Porter's testimony at the trial, Villiers and Walker got into a fight over the lion's share of the money they took when they knocked over the Fairpoint Savings & Loan."

Kelly lit the front corners of the balled-up paper with a single match. The dry kindling took the spark from the paper and began to crackle. "Sheriff Wray never found that money, did he?"

Matt Locke knelt in front of the fireplace and warmed his hands. "No, Sherlock, he didn't, and before you ask, no, I don't think it's hidden somewhere in this fishing cabin."

"I'm sure Frank Walker's daughters wasted many a fine-tooth comb on this place before selling it off."

"And you'd like me in my most paternal tones to assure you Villiers isn't heading this way to search the old place? Is that what you're listening for?"

At that moment the mountain lion snarled again, seeming even closer.

In the setting sun Camp Cochipimingo looked the same to Kelly as when she had tagged along with her father and his troop all those years ago. Six green tents surrounded a blazing fire, its flames illuminating a tall man in khaki shorts. He was speaking to a dozen or so scouts sitting around the burning logs and listening to his every word.

Kelly stood at the light's edge as her father introduced himself as an old scoutmaster now vacationing on the lake. The T-shirted leader extended his right hand to her father, who hesitated, then shook. The two chatted for a while before Matt Locke returned to where Kelly stood beside a flagpole and its still-flapping stars and stripes.

"Scoutmaster Warner's a little disappointed Porter couldn't make it, honey. Our sheriff must have quite a reputation as a storyteller. Anyway, Warner appreciates your offer, but he's taking the kids on a ten-mile hike tomorrow and wants them in the sack early."

Disappointed, she waved at the kids, then turned with her father to the now dimly lit path back to the cabin. "Did you tell him about Villiers?"

"Thought I'd better . . . just to be on the safe side. I really don't think he'd bother a group of kids, but Sam back there's a pretty big customer. He told me he could take care of his troop."

"Hey," called out the scoutmaster, "if you see Sheriff Wray, tell him to drop by this evening — just to check on us, you know."

"Sure thing," replied the Chief of Detectives.

The sheriff's Jeep was at their cabin when they arrived.

Even from a distance Kelly could see her old friend's face betrayed a mixture of relief and tension.

"No Villiers," concluded her father.

The sheriff looked tired as he said, "Old Byno only needed me to help him round up some strays that broke through his north fence. Heard that mountain lion screaming, if I don't miss my guess."

Kelly went into the cabin and brought him out a cup of steaming coffee. "Sheriff," she said as her night vision suddenly focused, "if you're still in the mood for rounding up, I'm pretty sure I can lead you to Villiers."

Both the sheriff and her father stared at the news anchor as if she were delivering the big story at the top of the hour.

The three of them crept down the pine-needled trail guided only by the light of the stars and the glow of smoldering embers. When they reached the edge of the clearing, the sheriff held up his hand and whispered, "I've got to do the rest of this myself."

Kelly and her father knelt behind a blueberry bush, watching as Sheriff Wray slipped through the grass and between several maples. From the rear he slowly approached the figure sitting on a log by the campfire.

"Heard you wanted to see me again, Villiers," said the sheriff without any nervousness.

Whirling to face the lawman's pistol, the T-shirted figure was so surprised he dropped a huge steel knife into the dirt. "How did you know?"

"Looks like you weren't a good scout, Reggie . . . you know, always prepared," he said. Motioning for Kelly and her father to join him, he called to the tents, "You boys can come out now. Everything's going to be just fine."

"If there were a merit badge for detection, honey," said her father as they approached the fire, "you'd have earned it tonight. Hey, boys, where's your real scoutmaster?"

As the boys pointed to a tent, Kelly headed back to the cabin with the sheriff's keys to drive back the Jeep. When she returned to the campsite, she found the real scoutmaster Warner rubbing his wrists that still looked pale from where a rope binding his hands had cut into his circulation.

"That guy had me scared," Warner was saying. "Walked into camp this morning with that huge Bowie knife of his. Told the boys he'd kill me if they didn't do what he wanted."

As the sheriff cuffed Villiers to the Jeep's roll bar, Kelly's attention turned toward the scouts. She marveled at their wrestling and joking with each other around what remained of the fire. Minutes earlier they had been in the presence of a killer, and now their horseplay suggested that the horror they had experienced was as meaningless as yesterday's newspaper. "Like most people around here," Kelly said, "Villiers knew sooner or later Sheriff Wray would be coming by to check on the troop. All he had to do was wait."

"In my clothes," added the scoutmaster. "But how did you know Villiers wasn't me? Your dad told me while you were fetching the sheriff's vehicle that neither of you had even seen a picture of him."

"Several things," answered the news anchor. "When he greeted my father, whom he knew was an old scoutmaster, he offered what most people do, his right hand, instead of the scouts' traditional left-handed clasp."

"The hand nearest the heart," added her father. "I noticed the mistake, but didn't think much of it. Figured he thought he was dealing with a civilian no matter what I said about my turn at scouting."

Kelly looked up at the flag still stirring in the night breeze. "There are only four spots where the flag flies continuously night and day, and Camp Cochipimingo isn't one of them."

"She sounds like the *Handbook* itself, said the scoutmaster."

"Sometimes," joked Matt Locke, "I think she should be the Chief of Detectives. She's like her idol. My Sherlock here notices things everybody else overlooks."

"Not always," Kelly said with a laugh. "In fact, Scoutmaster Warner, you owe your kids the greater credit."

"What do you mean?"

"When I started thinking about the discrepancies at the campsite, I remembered something earlier that should have alerted me. Hoping somebody who drove by the camp entrance would notice, your scouts were signaling your problem in a way they thought might alert someone without Villiers catching on."

"Signaling?"

"Three scouts were kneeling beside three standing next to three kneeling. Remember your Morse code?"

"How clever of them," said the scoutmaster with a satisfied grin. "Three short, three long, three short. S O S."

As Kelly and her father climbed into the Jeep, Sheriff Wray said, "Well, we broke a campfire tradition tonight. This is one scary story with a happy ending."

"So, Watson," posed Kelly to her father, do you think you and I will ever get a vacation from crime?"

Workout

by Jean Paiva

"**M**ake It Burn, Make It Really Burn," echoed in Jenny's head as she limped to the bus stop. Aside from her aching tendons (oh, those stretches), her obliques throbbed, deltoids pulsed, quadriceps seared, and gluteus maximus cried out in agony. The rest of her body merely suffered in silence, threatening a painful revolt should she move a fraction too far in any direction other than straight up and forward.

"It will be worth it; it will be worth it; it will be worth it," she chanted, taking small steps and feeling much like the "little engine that could." Already, only one month of thrice weekly sessions with the video tape recorder had noticeably diminished the massive outbreak of cellulite that normally blossomed like a wild fungus from her knees to her elbows.

First thing, before even going to the office, she would buy that brand new video tape — the one "guaranteed" to be more effective. Each of the just-introduced-and-completely-revised versions was tailored for a specific problem area! The one that focused on firm thighs was the priority. And maybe the one for slim waists. And — well, that should do for now.

Nothing, yet, had changed in her overall, over-stuffed sausage shape; but there was a blind confidence that this, too, would soon see a reversal of the ravages of time and eclairs. "Thirty-three," she cheerfully reminded herself, "is not yet over the hill."

The electronic bus sign flashed DOWNTOWN and, knowing the transport line's erratic schedule, rush hour or not, Jenny hobbled even quicker. A hitherto unknown group of muscles twinged their discord, but the good fairy of all workout buffs was looking over her shoulder as she slipped into the last vacant seat, allowed to blissfully ride for twenty minutes without . . . moving . . . a . . . muscle.

The typewriter, a newly purchased, computerized model, required little in the way of expended energy. Tap tap tapping the keys allowed Jenny to move only her fingers, not calling into action those abused biceps. Working carefully, even her wrists could remain immobile — that is, until tonight's session with the new video tape, now tucked safely under the desk. She had limited herself to just one — emphasis on thighs — and was proud of the restraint. George would also be proud.

St. Michaels Hospice Retail Ltd

Unit 1, Enviro21 Park, Queensway Avenue South, St. Leonards-on-Sea, East Sussex, TN38 9AG, United Kingdom

Shipping Address

Dennis McGuirk
48 SPRINGFIELD CLOSE
BURTON-ON-THE-WOLDS
LOUGHBOROUGH
LEICESTERSHIRE
LE12 5AN
United Kingdom

Order Number:	2910
Channel Ref:	26-10705-47121
Despatch Date:	30/10/2023

Qty	SKU	Name
1	Shelf D4 7509	Fishing For Bass With Bill & Bob - Angling Times 1966

Sighting a familiar group headed for the break area, Jenny absently realized that it was lunch time. The attention required not to move any more than absolutely necessary, while still staying productive, had taken every ounce of her concentration.

Time passed unheeded and soon forgotten. A cup of herbal tea, no caffeine to poison the body, would not only be refreshing but might loosen some of those neck knots. Despite the newly purchased, heated, orthopedic back cushion strapped to her chair, the pain threatened to cut off her breathing.

Carefully rising, not straining the upper or lower abdominals, Jenny slowly made her way to the sounds of laughter.

Led by her nose to the rich smell of freshly delivered pizza, forbidden and devoutly desired, the actual words being spoken didn't penetrate until she stood by the lunchroom door.

"It's a riot watching the blimp stagger around," a nasal voice belonging to Chris, one of the salesmen, rang through the open door. "She mentioned getting into shape but that implies you've got a shape to start with."

Raucous laughter flowed from the room like waves of sewer waste, each tide assailing Jenny's senses.

"When they handed out body types, she must have stood in the line for cows," another familiar voice echoed, launching a fresh bout of mirth.

"Give the kid a break," a man's gentle voice — thank you, Abe — cut in, apparently striving to gain control over his own laughter. "If your measurements sounded like they were in the metric system, you'd try to do something about it."

"Yeah, calling out her numbers sounds like a football play," yet another voice chimed in.

Chris the creep cut right back in, not wanting to be left out of this golden opportunity to rank and rile. "And even if she manages to get that potato sack bod into some semblance of a shape," he gasped between hoots, "what's she going to do with that potato face?"

Turning around, Jenny rode the riotous laughter back to the haven of her desk.

A cup of tea really wouldn't taste that good right now. Instead, a call to George was what her lunch break was really for — followed by a brisk walk to the grocer's for the proscribed apple and 37-calorie rice cake.

George, while many would not consider him handsome or even charming, was the best thing that had ever happened to Jenny. If she hadn't made that last minute decision to attend an anthropological lecture at the public library, this important part of her life would never have been. The missionary couple, a Dr. and Mrs. Cockles — their names would forever warm her heart — were fascinating with their photographs and slides. The thirty years they had spent in tribal living were under the most primitive circumstances; they were truly dedicated to have brought culture and civilization to the heathens. Leaving behind the Bible, Milton Berle, and Louis Auchincloss, they left the savages with true role models upon which a productive society could be built.

George's rapt attention during the lecture spoke volumes for his sensitivity and depth. A mere trace of what must have been a devastating bout of adolescent acne was transformed by his inner glow. His raincoat lay carefully folded on his lap; his only movement in the darkened room a slight shuddering of his right arm — apparently tremors betraying the deep, nearly religious, transmutation he was undergoing.

Dialing George's phone number, Jenny recalled the quiet and shy man fumbling, it would almost seem with his trousers, as she approached him after the lights were turned on. Shy and withdrawn, his eyes darting behind rather thick — but distinguished — horn-rimmed glasses, he'd barely been able to respond to her gentle query as to his enjoyment of the lecture.

Eventually she'd managed to elicit a crooked smile from him and the admission that he had reached new heights of ecstasy while listening to the aged couple recite their treks into primitive culture. George had shown the deepest admiration for how the missionaries had brought progress to those nude and needy people they showed so many, many nude slides of.

This intellectual summary of the Cockles profound sacrifice proved, on the spot, that here was a man of great sensitivity and potential. The crowing glory was when, after inviting him to her neat single room apartment he behaved like a perfect gentleman.

George did not make even the slightest advance on her in what others would consider advantageous circumstances.

His high-pitched voice, one she'd grown to find most pleasant when he whispered in her ear at the movie theater, answered on the third ring.

"George Alexander Philmartin, here. What may I do for you," the voice said, as cultured a way to respond as she could ever hope to hear.

"It's Jenny, George," she cooed into the phone, making sure no one was near enough to overhear.

"Oh, Jenny . . . ah, how are you," he thoughtfully queried, sounding somewhat — but that was impossible — preoccupied.

"Just fine, George. I was thinking about you and decided to be bold and surprise you with an invitation for dinner."

"Dinner? Oh dear, this is rather short notice."

Somewhere in his background Jenny heard giggles. Smiling to herself she thought of the various daytime dramas he would be watching and decided on *All My Children* as appropriate to the time of day.

"How's Erica doing today," Jenny politely inquired.

"Erica who?" George sounded nervous.

"Erica on television, of course," Jenny sweetly replied.

"The TV's not on," George said, the giggles in his background growing louder and sounding even closer to the phone.

"Oh, you must be . . . ," Jenny began, thinking of the radio, as words from a very female voice transmitted over the open phone line.

"Georgie worgie, puddin', and pie, come back to little Lisa, or you're gonna make her cry."

"Shut up," a voice that sounded like George's hissed — apparently turned away from the phone but nonetheless absolutely and clearly transmitted into the earpiece held, with trembling fingers, by Jenny.

"Jenny, my dear," this voice — definitely belonging to George — addressed her, "I'm — ah — a little tied up right now," a statement which was met with a renewed torrent of giggles in the background. "Perhaps I can call you later, at home, this evening, and we can chat."

Her voice deserting her, her stomach feeling like it had been kicked by a mule from the inside out — which couldn't be attributed to the exercise regime — and her very breath robbed from her lungs by a failure in automatic respiratory responses, Jenny managed to agree to talk later and hung up the phone.

Being left out of the office party at 5:30 (every last employee except Jenny was going) celebrating a major sale to a industry giant was unimportant. What mattered was getting home and switching on her prized video tape recorder, plugging in the new exercise tape, and working out. Someday, soon, when she was svelte and shapely they'd be sorry. All of them.

The commute home mirrored the morning trip in; moving too quickly for a bus just arrived, wreaking havoc with abused muscles and tendons, and garnering the last seat even if it meant elbowing a frail old lady out of the way.

Home was where the heart was. It didn't need fancy curtains or a new bedspread or even a living creature — fish, birds, or cats were a nuisance — to make it a welcome sight. The bare walls, devoid of even a calendar, might need painting but the linoleum floor was bright and shiny, newly waxed so that Jenny could exercise mirrored in the gleam from below. All furniture — the single bed, the small dresser, the tiny table, and two straight-back chairs — had been moved back to make room for the shiny, new, chrome television-stand proudly bearing a brand-new color 13" television and bottom-of-the-line model VCR.

Shrugging out of her simple, shapeless sheath dress, which she filled from shoulder to hem, Jenny quickly blended her vegetable drink. The pre-digested dinner consumed, she donned her terry-cloth shorts and matching tank top. After tearing the shrink-wrapped plastic from the new tape cassette, Jenny reverently inserted the cartridge in the already activated unit.

She was ready.

As the background music rose over the opening credits, Jenny shook out her arms and legs. The smiling face of her fearless leader, surrounded by perfectly coiffed hair and a body the instructor promised "could be yours" if you just stayed with her for 35 minutes of torture a day, turned to the camera. Anticipating the welcome opening words, "Are you ready? . . ." Jenny was nonplussed when the smile on her idol's face fell and those warm and twinkling brown eyes glassed over.

"Oh, no; it's you again," the television transmitted. "What did I do to deserve this?"

"But I'm ready," Jenny said. "Aren't you going to ask if I'm ready?"

"Honey, no matter how ready you are, it's still hopeless," the small but perfectly proportioned image shot back. "I don't promise miracles, just a toned body. He was right, you know."

"Who was right?" Jenny asked, her lower lip now trembling.

"The guy at your office who said you have to have a shape to start with. What you've got doesn't qualify. It's hopeless, so just give up."

"But I want to try!" Jenny pleaded, the trembling lip now threatening to vibrate her entire body. "Please, you're the only hope I've got. You've got to help me."

A glimmer of a smile touched the image's face. Perfectly shaped eyebrows raised in mock appraisal of the situation. "I think you're right," the television said, "I'm probably your only hope."

"You really are," Jenny whimpered.

"All right," the figure brusquely said, signaling for the background music to begin again, "but there's only one way I can think of to help you and you'll have to follow my every instruction to the letter or it won't work."

"Oh, I will, I will," Jenny answered, relieved and heartened at this new-found chance.

"Stand with your feet a little more than hip distance apart, chin up, stomach in, buttocks tight," the voice instructed.

Jenny carefully followed every movement.

"We're going to try something new."

"Oh, joy," whispered Jenny to the woman on the tiny screen, "I'll do anything you ask."

"Here we go," the woman answered. "Oh, and I won't be exercising along with you this time. I want to make sure you do it right."

"Anything you say," Jenny promised.

"Reach your arms way up, that's right, shoulders forward. Right arm over your right ear, no — hips are squared, stretch out. Good. Now left arm over your left ear. Good. Stretch — out. Both arms up and pull all the way down, as far as you can, between your legs. Further, pull further! Reach from the crown of your head to the floor. Reach! Reach! That's better. Hold that position.

"Bend your knees, stretch, don't bounce . . . breathe . . . press your head and arms through your legs, touch your chin to your chest, further! Make it Burn! No — stay in that position, Jenny; don't straighten up. Now, bend your right knee up in front of you and reach your left leg behind you as far as you can — further! — hips are pressed forward, feel that stretch! Make it Burn! Keep your head down. Move your right knee over your head and bring your left leg up from the back to cross over . . ."

The resulting crack was loud enough to startle Jenny's upstairs neighbor who made a mental note to knock on Jenny's door the next time she went out — Thursday, maybe — to ask her what broke.

"Bye bye Jenny," the television lady said as she reached out toward the rewind button. "If you can breathe for more than five minutes with your knee in your windpipe, I'll be amazed. And, with a broken back, I just don't see how you'll get out of that position."

A single tear welled up in Jenny's right eye.

"Believe me," the woman said just before she rewound, "it's the only solution."   ✗

MAYHEM IN ST MARGARET MEDE

by Peter King

"**K**eep that window closed!" shouted John Strode. "The smoke's all coming in!"

"Oh, don't be such a fussbudget!" Ella Neel had to shout as she leaned out of the train window. "You can see St Margaret Mede! Look!" Her words were drowned out by the shrill shriek of the whistle and the steely scrape of the wheels as the brakes clamped them down on the rails.

"Anyway, it's dangerous to lean out of a train window while the locomotive is pulling you along at sixty miles an hour," John Strode protested. He was aware that his words were lost, but he always felt obliged to restrain his headstrong young colleague whose disregard for danger got them into trouble so frequently.

Strode rose and collected his bowler hat, his umbrella, and his suitcase from the overhead rack. He had to steady himself as the train slowed. Then with a lurch and a final tooth-nerve grinding of metal, they came to a stop at the tiny village station.

"We're five minutes late," Strode said testily. "What time did we leave Paddington?"

"Four fifty," said Mrs Neel.

"That's very significant."

"Really? Why?"

"It proves that trains don't arrive in St Margaret Mede on time."

St Margaret Mede was apparently not a popular destination for they were the only passengers to alight.

"Over here," said Strode and they walked to the station-master who stood by the platform exit. He seemed amazed to see anyone get off the train, held their tickets close to his eyes to make sure they had the right station and clipped them.

"Can we have our return portions back?" asked Mrs Neel sweetly. He reluctantly handed them over.

"I wonder why he didn't think we would need them?" was Strode's murmured conjecture.

The High Street in St Margaret Mede was strangely quiet. John Strode and Ella Neel surveyed it with practiced eyes. "Are you thinking what I'm thinking?" murmured Mrs Neel.

" 'The quintessential English village,' " quoted Strode.

"That's what the Cotswold Bureau of Tourism calls it."

"So where is everybody?"

The butcher's shop across the street looked open, but it appeared to be empty of customers and staff. The flower shop had a dazzling array of colours in boxes and trays but it appeared unattended. So did the other shops. "Even the betting shop," Mrs Neel said, frowning.

Strode pointed his umbrella at the The Blue Boar that was next to The Novelty Shop. The red, black, and gold sign outside the pub looked new and shiny, while baskets of daisies and dandelions glistened from recent watering.

"We may as well register and get rid of these suitcases," Strode said. "Then we can look around."

"Easier said than done," Mrs Neel muttered as Strode rapped on the desk for the fourth time. Eventually, a very large lady in a faded apron appeared. "Was there something?" she asked belligerently.

"We'd like to register," said Strode with an easy smile. He gave their names. The lady stared at them. "Two rooms?" she questioned after looking at a sheet before her.

Half an hour later, John Strode and Ella Neel met in the bar. It was empty. "Strange," said Mrs Neel. "Where is that pleasing thump of darts hitting a cork board?"

"Not to mention the happy clink of glasses and the landlord's cheery, 'First one's on the house.'"

They departed the unwelcoming atmosphere of the Blue Boar. "Still no-one on the streets," Mrs Neel observed. "Most odd. Could it be the population is afraid?"

"Afraid of what?" Mrs Neel's long-legged stride kept up with her companion effortlessly as they walked along the empty sidewalk.

"You recall our mission?" Strode said. "The reason the Ministry sent us here? St Margaret Mede has had sixteen murders, twelve robberies, eight muggings, two cases of embezzlement, three blackmails, two poison-pen campaigns, and four missing persons."

"Three missing persons," Mrs Neel corrected. "Just before we left, a report came in that a body had been found in the village pond."

"Drowned?"

"No. Stabbed and poisoned."

"But drowned afterward surely?"

"Well, yes. At least she would have been if she hadn't already been stabbed and poisoned."

"She?"

"Yes, the victim was the village constable. St Margaret Mede prides itself on being in the vanguard of equal rights for women."

"H'm," said Strode, "no wonder the populace is afraid."

They stopped at a store front. The print on the large window said WINSTONE FUNERAL PARLOR. "Look!" said Strode. He pointed to an elaborate wreath. It was the only object in the window. A prominent card declared:

RIP
John Strode

"Is that a date in the corner?" asked Strode faintly.

"Yes," said Mrs Neel. "It's today's date. Isn't that a coincidence?"

"I hope so," Strode said.

A newsagent shop was ahead of them. Mrs Neel plucked the top copy from the stack of newpapers on the rack and opened it to display the headline. "Looks like we're famous," she observed wryly as they read:

TWO MINISTRY CLERKS DIE IN COTSWOLD VILLAGE

"Clerks!" snorted John Strode.

"Our cover must be blown," said Ella Neel.

"Today's date," commented Strode. "*The Daily Gazette* is really on top of the news."

"Premature, I'd call it," said Mrs Neel.

"I'd prefer erroneous," said Strode.

A sudden roar startled them. It rose to a bellow and a motorcycle swept around the corner, bounced up on to the sidewalk and headed directly for them. Years of training and experience paid off as the two of them quickly stepped away from one another. The split second of indecision by the black-helmeted driver caused the black torpedo to race between them instead of pushing them through the newsagent's window. As it slewed around, another attack was clearly contemplated, but the front wheel swerved and the cycle thundered down the High Street and out of sight.

Strode motioned toward the newspaper still in Mrs Neel's hand. "Does that account say, 'Hurled through shop window'?"

"No, it says, 'Died in the stocks'."

"Stocks?" frowned Strode but Mrs Neel tossed the paper nonchalantly into a trash barrel and the two continued their walk. They stayed away from the inside of the sidewalk where they were vulnerable to items dropped from rooftops but also away from the edge of the sidewalk.

A cheery "Good afternoon!" startled them. They turned to see a figure in clerical garb on an old Raleigh bicycle.

"Good afternoon, vicar!" Strode prided himself on getting along well with the clergy and Mrs Neel indulged him. The vicar stopped, one foot on the ground, hands still on the handlebars. "Quiet today," Strode called out, "Is it always like this?"

"Goodness gracious, no," said the vicar, "in fact, it's occasionally noisy and sometimes, well, even violent." He was elderly with a lined face and a suitably pious air.

"We hope it won't be violent for the next few days," said Strode.

"There's no telling." The vicar shook his head in dismay. "Just no telling."

"The nearest we've seen to violence so far has been a person on a motorcycle and in a great hurry," said Mrs Neel.

"And with a blurred idea of the difference between a road and a pavement," added Strode.

"That would be Letitia," the vicar sighed. "A headstrong girl."

"She'll be headless, too, if she always drives like that," said Mrs Neel.

"I've spoken to her," the vicar said. "So has Primrose."

"Primrose being . . . ?" Mrs Neel prompted.

"Our village constable."

"Really? We thought Primrose was, er — incapacitated?"

"Not when I saw her earlier this morning," the vicar said. He looked from one to the other of the faces of the two visitors to St Margaret Mede. "Oh, I see, you're thinking of Rosemary, the last village constable. Oh, no, Primrose is our new one."

"Rosemary, yes," Strode said. "What exactly did happen to her?"

"Poor Rosemary, one gin too many, I'm afraid. We really should put up a fence around the village pond. Other unfortunates may fall in, too."

"Is that what happened to her?" asked Mrs Neel. "Drowned?"

"So sad." The vicar looked distressed. "There is only two feet of water in it, too."

"How about the Vicarage?" asked Mrs Neel. "Is all well there? No incidents?"

"Oh, no," the vicar smiled.

"No murders?"

"Murder at the Vicarage? Good heavens, no." He frowned.

"What have you heard?"

"Must have been something I read," responded Mrs Neel sweetly. "Good morning, vicar."

He nodded, tipped his hat and cycled off, looking around anxiously for non-existent cars.

"YE OLDE TEA ROOMS AND CAFÉ," Strode read the sign, peering in the window past the lace curtain. "Not a tea-drinker in sight. Not a waitress in sight, either."

"You're thinking that St Margaret Mede is in need of a more vigourous hand at the helm of the Department of Tourism?" asked Mrs Neel.

"The thought had crossed my mind," Strode admitted.

"Still, they keep it very clean and tidy."

"No wonder, there's no one to dirty it."

"Listen!" said Strode abruptly and they both stopped. The throaty splutter of a small motor had started nearby.

"Another motorcycle?" Mrs Neel asked.

"Not powerful enough, not even for a scooter. It's coming from down here."

'Down there' was a narrow alley, cobble-stoned and with a row of neat cottages on each side. Window boxes held dazzling displays of fresh cut flowers. Door handles and letter box slots gleamed from a recent application of Brasso.

Their footsteps echoed sharply. They could see no one, but the alley was short and they came out into an area of green and grey. The expanse of well-tended, carefully cut grass was broken up in irregular fashion by aging tombstones. A path leading to an old church was flanked by a twin hedgerow.

The source of the sound was a big man in a leather apron. He was wielding a portable hedge clipper like a Crusader swinging a sword. He had greying hair and a scowl on his face as if he were chopping down Saracens.

Strode and Mrs Neel exchanged glances, then approached him warily. He became aware of them but continued his task.

They came closer, then close enough that he could not ignore them.

"Beautiful day!" Strode called out cheerfully as the gardener flicked off the switch and the sound died.

"You keep the cemetery looking immaculate, I must say," Ella Neel congratulated him.

The man stood immobile, belligerent. He looked from one to the other.

"Graveyard," he said in an appropriately sepulchral voice. "It's a graveyard."

Strode was scrutinizing tombstones. "Several generations

of villagers here, I see."

"Not just villagers," the gardener grunted. "Some visitors, too. Tourists, a lot of 'em."

Strode turned a jovial smile on him. "Ah, yes, there was one a couple of months ago, I recall. Poor chap got himself decapitated and dismembered. Very messily, too. Don't remember just what the coroner concluded. Some kind of a high-speed cutting tool — with serrated edges, wasn't it?"

The gardener changed his grip on the hedge trimmer. He said nothing.

"Wasn't that just a couple of weeks after that woman fell from the church tower?" asked Mrs Neel brightly.

The gardener jerked his head in the direction of the grey building behind him. "Aye, she fell on that pavement there. Splattered her brains all over."

"Ah, the blood-stained pavement," Strode said. "So that's where that fits."

"Dear me," murmured Mrs Neel. "Poor Annabella. So that's why she never wrote home to Mother."

"You knew her?" The gardener's beetling brows beetled even closer.

"A business acquaintance," said Mrs Neel. They nodded to the gardener and strolled on.

"At least, the Ministry will be relieved to hear that Annabella didn't defect," she said to Strode who was looking at his watch.

"Four o'clock; shall we try the tea room again? I could do with a cuppa."

Inside the lace curtained windows of Ye Olde Tea Rooms and Café, a very elderly lady eventually answered their repeated calls. "All right, all right, I'm coming. I've got to wash the saucers, haven't I?" She had a coarse craggy face and a confrontational manner.

From a tiny table, Strode and Mrs Neel studied the walls with their photographs and posters. One section had a pattern of book covers. Mrs Neel leaned forward. "They are all by Joan Marble. Of course, she lives here."

" 'The Queen of Crime,' they call her." Strode nodded.

"That's right, she does." He pointed. " 'The most popular mystery writer of the century,' it says on the cover of *The Six Clocks Mystery.*"

"I wonder if she could help us," mused Mrs Neel.

"Remember when she disappeared a while ago?" Strode asked. "Did it ever come out where she went and why?"

"Not that I recall."

The elderly waitress returned with two cups and saucers, which she slapped down with only a minimum of splashing. "Two hawthorn teas."

"But I ordered comfrey tea," Mrs Neel objected.

"And I ordered myrtle tea," said Strode.

"We're out. Only got hawthorn left," said the waitress and hobbled away.

They sipped hawthorn tea. "That sounds interesting," Strode said, aiming a finger at a poster advertising the village museum. 'The Story of St Margaret Mede — Ten Centuries Brought to Life,' it proclaimed.

"Warm in here," muttered Mrs Neel.

"M'm," agreed Strode. "Let's finish the tea and get out into the fresh air." They did so and Strode scattered coins on the table when the waitress failed to respond to calls.

The air outside felt warm and oppressive. "Should have drunk black coffee," Strode commented.

"I suppose that's appropriate, too," said Mrs Neel.

The museum was on the next corner and a sign said OPEN. The front was unprepossessing, but the two suits of armour inside the entrance stood like guards, swords at the ready. Strode and Mrs Neel walked in past the unattended ticket booth.

"St Margaret Mede sent men to the Crusades," said a printed panel and maps showed their route. Rusty weapons hung on the walls, and a Crusader banner, tattered and dirty, hung limply. They walked on, past 1400 and 1500.

"After 1600," said the panel, "village life was influenced by religious differences. Witch trials had been conducted and the guilty condemned. Some had been drowned in the village pond and some had been stoned to death in the stocks."

Mrs Neel and John Strode exchanged looks. "Stocks!" they said in unison. Strode passed a hand over his brow. "I feel — faint," he whispered. Mrs Neel flashed a look of surprise at him, but her step faltered and she gasped, "So do I. That tea . . ."

It was dark and only a few moonbeams slanted in through high windows. The silence was intense. It was broken by the village church bell tolling six o'clock. A bird chirped, the kind of early morning chirpiness that can be really irritating.

Strode's uncertain voice asked, "Mrs Neel, are you all right?"

"Just going to ask you that. Can you move your hands and arms?"

"No," came after a moment of heavy breathing.

The moonbeams tilted closer and reflected off a shield on

the wall, one of the few items to enjoy the advantage of polish. Both saw their predicament at once.

"We're in the stocks."

There was a moment of assessment by both agents.

"Think we're going to be stoned?" asked Strode.

"No," said Mrs Neel. "These people — whoever they are — seem to be more efficient than that. They disposed of Rosemary in the pond. Hector — they took care of him — he went all to pieces . . . "

"Hector's Tarot should have warned him not to listen to old saws," said Strode.

"While poor Annabella didn't fall from the church steeple — "

"She was pushed."

Silence prevailed while both reviewed their training.

"I don't remember a session on escaping from stocks," Mrs Neel grumbled.

The streams of light moved on from the shield. It was now on the wall almost over their heads. Strode was straining his neck to look over his shoulder.

"See that large executioner's axe up there?"

"Yes, massive thing. You could cleave an ox with that axe."

"It's only suspended by one bit of rope."

Mrs Neel twisted her neck further. "You're not thinking what I think you're thinking, are you?'

"Have a better idea?"

"I have a thin bladed knife strapped high on my thigh."

"Oh, my!"

Mrs Neel ignored the innuendo — if that's what it was.

"If I can squirm around — just a —" There was rustling and scraping in the darkness.

"Keep me informed," said Strode.

A gasp of frustration came. "No. Can't reach up there."

"Perhaps if I edge closer, I can —"

"I don't think so," Mrs Neel said coldly. "You're in a different stock — or is it stocks?"

"That's it, then. We're back to the axe. We have to dislodge it. If we shake hard, we might rock these stocks. The action might loosen the axe."

"And the axe might fall and knock off my block," said Mrs Neel.

"It's our only chance. I'm willing to risk it — bravely."

"Stout fellow," said Mrs Neel dourly and began to rock.

"Hey, wait a minute! I meant both at the same —" Strode joined her hastily.

The creaking and groaning grew louder, some of it coming from the stocks that seemed older than they looked.

"More!" gasped Strode.

"Look out!" called Mrs Neel, "it's falling!"

An almighty crash followed and a sound of splintering wood. Then came a crunch and a splitting noise.

"Strode! Are you still alive?"

"Yes," he answered faintly, "I'm just in two halves."

The moon, hitherto obliging, had gone, but in its place was the first light of dawn. It revealed Strode lying on his side, struggling to free himself from shattered wooden remnants.

For a moment, he paused, exhausted. "Listen," said Ella Neel. Noises came from afar. "Someone's coming in!"

Strode renewed his efforts and at last an arm was free. He pulled away pieces of wood from the other arm and stood. "Me next," said Mrs Neel and he used the axe to lever the imprisoning wood blocks loose.

When the lights flickered on in the museum, two men and a woman came in. They crossed the room, passed the Iron Maiden and the Court Executioner. They stopped, staring at the litter of wood pieces on the floor.

"Where are they?" asked the woman. "You fools! You should have taken care of them last night!"

The three came forward hesitantly.

"Find them!" the woman snapped. The two men went past the rack and the thumbscrews, past the black-hooded cluster of the Spanish Inquisition and paused. The door of the Iron Maiden swung open with a clang, and Mrs Neel sprang out and swung a high kick at the nearest man. The toe of her shoe connected satisfyingly under his chin and there was a sound like crushing a coconut.

Simultaneously, the Court Executioner came to life and his robes swirled as the axe that had played a major supporting rôle in the escape described a flashing arc. Strode used it in reverse — fortunately for its recipient — so that instead of severing his head, the flat surface thunked against the back of his cranium and stretched him out, unconscious at the very least.

The elderly waitress from Ye Olde Tea Rooms no longer looked so old and certainly not infirm. The snarl might have intimidated others as she crouched into a martial arts stance and moved her hands as if she were molding invisible clay.

"Ha!" she growled.

Ella Neel made no reply to that. She simply did a treble cartwheel and made sure that the dazzling maneuver concluded with one elbow thrusting deep into the other's throat. It had the impact of a steam hammer and was followed immediately by a powerful knee in the groin and a hammer punch to the carotid artery. The older woman, clearly incapacitated, collapsed like a sack of elderflowers.

Strode looked on with disappointment clear on his face. "Aren't these fights supposed to last longer?"

"Probably," said Mrs Neel negligently, "but she annoyed me — I mean, she did bring me the wrong tea."

The pockets of the prostrate trio yielded nothing of any value; and when Strode and Mrs Neel left the museum, three well-trussed bodies occupied wall niches in the mausoleum room. In the entry hall, though, were a few copies of the *St Margaret Mede Newsletter*, a free newspaper of a dozen pages. Among the exciting events being promoted were a spelling bee, a domino competition, and a show of quilts knitted by the members of the Ladies Institute. Ella Neel was about to toss it away after this perusal when she stopped. "Look at this, Strode!"

She read aloud the item in the lower half of the third page that had caught her eye. " 'Our own Miss Joan Marble will conduct another of her instructional seminars in her cottage across from the Vicarage.' "

She frowned. "Unfortunately, it was two days ago."

"Pity," said Strode. "Still, we know where she lives. At least that means we won't have to ask directions. I suspect that could be a very hazardous procedure in this environment."

"I'm hungry," said Mrs Neel, "But I fear that seeking breakfast might be equally perilous. I have an idea, though —"

"Fire away."

"There'll be no service in Ye Olde Tea Rooms and Café —" Mrs Neel indicated the largest and oldest of the inert forms in the wall niches, "— so if we go there, we may have to cook our own."

"It may also be a good temporary hideout until we go to seek the help of the no doubt estimable Miss Marble. Good thinking, Mrs N — by the way, have you read any of her books?"

"Yes, they're quite clever, actually. Rural crime novels. The crimes are solved by a demure old lady called Amanda Crisbie."

"They take place in a village, I suppose?"

"Yes, rather like this one. Oddly enough, no new books have appeared in print since Joan Marble's disappearance and return."

The pantry of the Ye Olde Tea Rooms and Café contained various healthy potions such as acorn coffee and yerba mate. Ella Neel's nose wrinkled in critical comment, but she brewed one cup of each. On dainty blue-and-white plates, she piled St John's Wort rolls, Butcher's Broom buns, and parsleyed oat cakes. A dish of alfalfa butter and some sunflower jam completed this original breakfast.

Strode eyed the festive array with some skepticism. "I was rather looking forward to sausages and black pudding."

"I think I saw some wortleberry muffins —"

"Never mind," Strode said.

"If we were nearer the sea, there'd be some seaweed scones —"

"These will do," Strode said, reaching for another bun.

The absence of staff was clearly not noticed by any of the village inhabitants, because none of the latter appeared. Mrs Neel, who always liked to be tidy, cleaned the table and restored the jars and utensils to their places. They went out into the silent street where the sidewalks were empty.

"Perhaps they've all been poisoned by health foods," said Strode.

"You're just bad-tempered because you didn't get your sausages. In this village, you might be better off without them. I mean, you'd never know who might be in them."

Across from the vicarage, Miss Marble's cottage had roses round the door.

The whitish stone doorstep had been recently scrubbed, the windows were clean, and the trim around them was freshly painted white.

No one answered the bell.

"Out doing her shopping?" pondered Mrs Neel.

"Possible. I wonder if she locks the door when she goes . . ."

Miss Marble did not. They went in to a parlour with flowered wallpaper, antimacassars, a high mantelpiece with Toby jugs, and a rag rug on the linoleum floor. Potted ferns and vases of cut roses vied for space with postcards from the seaside and faded photographs in tortoise-shell frames on shelves in the corners.

Strode was inspecting the postcards. "One from the Caribbean," he commented, "and this place looks familiar — ah, yes, it's from Bertram's Hotel; they hope she'll return and they enjoyed her visit." He picked up another that showed the Sphinx. "Taken from the Nile steamer," he murmured, "and this one — h'm, Miss Crisbie has friends among the nobility — it's from

Lord Edgeware." Mrs Neel came over to join him.

"Thought he was dead," she said. They examined more cards.

"Not presumably when this was written —"

Strode was interrupted by a voice from behind him.

"My dears, I'm so glad you're making yourselves at home —"

Joan Marble was the archtypical elderly spinster. She had white hair, a gentle voice, and placid, china-blue eyes.

"The door was unlocked," explained Strode, "so we decided to wait."

"I'm so glad you did. Please sit down, we have so much to talk about. Would you like a cup of tea?"

They all sat. Strode and Mrs Neel exchanged brief glances. "Ah, no thank you," Mrs Neel said. "We had one at Ye Olde Tea Rooms —"

"— and Café," contributed Strode. "Didn't agree with us."

Miss Marble shook her white head sadly. "I've told Beatrice to be careful where she picks those hawthorn blossoms. There's a plant called Devilweed, it grows in the churchyard and it looks just like hawthorn."

"It probably knocks people out," Mrs Neel said cheerfully.

"Why, yes. Do you know it?"

"You could say that," Mrs Neel agreed.

"They say that a second cup has been known to kill people."

"Good thing we didn't stay for seconds," said Strode briskly. "Still writing about Amanda Crisbie, are you?"

"Oh, yes." Miss Marble beamed. "She's very much a part of me, you know. Well, so much, in fact, that I seem to be a part of her."

"A very observant woman," Mrs Neel said. "But then, so are you, I'm sure."

"One gets to know so much about human nature, living in a village," said Miss Marble. "There is a great deal of wickedness in village life, you know. I hope you will never come to realize just how wicked."

"The lowest and vilest alleys in London do not present a more dismal record of sin than does the smiling and beautiful English countryside," intoned Strode and Mrs Neel shot him a surprised look. "Why, Strode, how observant of you!"

"Not me. Sherlock Holmes said that."

"What a pity that nothing has appeared in print since your — er, disappearance." Mrs Neel smiled brightly at Miss Marble.

"It's true I haven't had anything new published —"

"Busy with other endeavours, no doubt," Strode nodded.

Miss Marble's appearance underwent a change, subtle but

obvious to the trained eye of the Ministry agents. She was more alert, more formidable — and less the gentle old lady.

"Tell me," Strode went on in his genial manner, "these instructional seminars of yours. Cover a wide range of topics, do they?"

"Indeed they do." Miss Marble was still affable but with a stitched edge of caution. "The villagers say they benefit from them immensely."

"And not just the villagers." said Mrs Neel. "You have many postcards from grateful clients all over the country."

"But not, I notice, from any of our prisons," supplied Strode.

"Prisons?" The question was toneless.

"Yes, where many of your clients reside. Not enough, really, you train your people well. You've been training criminals in every aspect of criminality since you disposed of the real Miss Marble and then came here to take her place. You couldn't write like her but you could teach criminals, and your own crew of cutthroats eliminated agent after agent who came here to find out why St Margaret Mede had more than its fair share of crime."

Miss Marble nodded softly. "I did get a little concerned that we were stretching the statistical net. Perhaps I should have been more restrictive."

"Hard to resist the lure of expanding a profitable business," Mrs Neel said. "So now we must —"

Miss Marble came out of the chair and crossed the room with an agility that astonished the two from the Ministry. She pulled open the door, swept through the gate and out on to the pavement where she put two fingers in her mouth and let out a shrill and most unladylike whistle.

A familiar-looking black motorcycle came roaring down the street and screeched to a shuddering stop. Strode and Mrs Neel stared in amazement at Miss Marble's agility as she leaped on to the pillion seat and thumped a fist on the driver's back. As the two hurried forward to intercept, the goggled and helmeted rider wrenched the throttle and swung the nose of the cycle in their direction. The front wheel lifted off the ground as the vehicle raced at them.

Again, the training of the Ministry agents paid off and, separating swiftly, they received only glancing blows, which, nevertheless, sent them sprawling.

The cycle, rocking and bouncing from the double impact, lost momentum temporarily, then its engine screamed as, swinging around, it came at them determined to complete its murderous task on the two agents laying on the pavement.

Strode felt a jab of pain in his right elbow but it also served to remind him that his Ministry-equipment umbrella was still firmly clenched in that hand. As the cycle hurtled toward them, he rolled to one side and thrust the high-strength steel tip between the spokes of the rear wheel. The stalled engine protested with a banshee wail, and the bike slithered along on one side, flinging out a spray of sparks. The two riders were flung off like rag dolls, and the bike crashed into Miss Marble's picket fence, erupting a fountain of white stakes.

The Ministry agents climbed to their feet and each examined a body. They looked at each other and shook their heads.

"Nemesis!" Mrs Neel called out. She ran to the cycle, righted it and jumped on, Strode immediately after her.

Japanese engineering snarled triumphantly, and they thundered out of St Margaret Mede as a church bell pealed a farewell. ✗